THE SOC

ERIN MC LUCKIE MOYA

For those who have been hindered and moulded in a thousand ways through choices that are not their own. We see you, support you and love you.

TRIGGER WARNINGS

Although this is a work of fiction, this book tackles hard-to-swallow topics.
These include:
Rape
Human trafficking
Child trafficking
Prostitution
Control through Society

Contents

CHAPTER ONE : THE MESSAGE

I tapped my all-star clad foot against the pebbled pavement, sipping on my ice tea crush, waiting at our usual table for Kerri to arrive.

I shouldn't be annoyed. Not really - we all *know* how she is, and yet despite that - despite me agreeing to this meeting knowing that she'd be late - the irritation surged through me, leaving me grappling for control of my own damn emotions.

Schooling my expression, I sat at the steel white table on the sidewalk, sipping my ice tea, looking bored.

My phone vibrated against the table, and I suppressed the urge to roll my eyes. If she was cancelling on me, I would kill her. Okay - *kill* may be a tad dramatic, but I was certainly annoyed.

Mom: Honey - are you sure?

I read the message and huffed out a breath. It's not as if I had much of a choice. All that would happen is that I would push the inevitable out by a few months or a year, but eventually I would have to commit.

Illuminati. The word clanged through my brain, jangling my senses in a way that had my hairs standing on end. It was a word that was passed around the dinner table in hushed tones. We mostly referred to it as "The Society", and my parents, grandparents, and great-grandparents were all a part of it, sowing the seeds of the organisation, building it to a larger reach day by day.

For the most part, we didn't have an active role in it. Well, at least I *think* we didn't. I knew that things came easily to us - I wasn't completely oblivious. I knew that my father's business was successful - probably more than what it should be, *and* I managed to get into the University of my choice fairly seamlessly.

And, despite my family's involvement with The Society, they had shielded me for the most part. Sure, I knew that we had ties to them, but it did not directly impact my life in the slightest.

The catch to The Society nudging the wheel of fortune turning in our favour? Each generation had to give three months of their adult life to The Society. No one really spoke about what they did when they were there, but the piecemeal conversation I had heard was filled with nostalgia - similar to summer camp stories. It made me feel a bit better about my situation.

There were a lot of conspiracy theories surrounding The Society, and in many ways I liked that about them - it gave them a cloak and dagger reputation, and I supposed it was intentional.

One of the conspiracy theories that was actually pretty close to the truth was The Society's logo - the all-seeing eye. It really was supposed to speak of truth, and how truth will always be seen by those who choose to look. Of course, the conspiracy theory distorted that, but it was eerie how close the world had actually come to knowing about us.

In jest, Natalia and I went to Greece one year and tattooed the evil eye on our wrists. It was a way of poking fun at the world while still being inconspicuous. Well, at least we thought so.

Natalia was one of my childhood friends, our parents ran in the same circles and she was obviously part of The Society.

My fingers deftly flew across my screen as I typed.

Aria: I'm sure mom.

Regardless, I needed to commit three months - one summer - of my life to The Society and then I would be free. So, it made sense to do it after graduation. At least this way, when I re-entered the world, it would be to start a job and become a productive member. I couldn't imagine building a life and career for myself and then having to pause it all simply to commit to The Society for three months. No, this way was better. A few of the other Society kids had done the same, and it seemed to work out for them.

"You will never believe what happened to me!" Kerri draped herself in the chair opposite mine dramatically.

"Oh?" I asked, arching an eyebrow.

"It looks like I got the internship at Molton Tech!" She squealed, clapping her hands in glee.

I dipped my head in acknowledgement.

"It took forever!" She continued, "I had to go through four rounds of interviews just to get this internship. *Internship* Aria. An *Internship*. Not a science posting. Not a full-time job - an *Internship.*"

Kerri wasn't a Society brat. She worked for everything she had, and somehow did not begrudge me for all I had without having to put in half the work. Or perhaps she didn't notice?

"Yeah, but you said that all these hoops you needed to jump through were worth it, because - and I quote 'from Molton Tech I'll be hired anywhere'."

She shrugged, "Yeah, you're right. It just feels so final now that I actually have the internship."

I smiled at her, waiting for her to continue.

"And," she continued dramatically, "I just found out that Ajax SinClaire won't even be there! And he was half the reason I applied for this damn position."

I laughed, spluttering ice tea everywhere.

"You have got to be kidding me?" I grinned, "You applied for this job thinking that the CEO of this billionaire organisation would be there during summer?"

"Hoped," she corrected. "I simply *hoped* that he would be around. I mean, everything I'd read about him says that he's a hard worker."

"And a playboy," I offered.

"Exactly," she nodded her head with a gleam in her eye, and I couldn't help but laugh once more.

"So, are you and Natalia heading out for one last hurrah in Europe before actually joining the real world like the rest of us plebs?" Kerri asked.

So, she wasn't as oblivious to our privilege as she seemed.

"Nope," I smiled, shrugging her comment off. "My dad has asked me to intern at his company this summer and Nats is taking this time off with her boyfriend."

"You're also interning?" she asked, aghast.

I shrugged. "Yeah, but I'm not sure which office he's stationing me at - it could be the London office though."

"Oh," her shoulders sagged.

This was my cover, because I couldn't very well tell Kerri that I was going to one of The Society's camps for three months. So, this was the best I could come up with.

"And do you have a job lined up for when you get back?" She asked.

"I'm supposed to be working for Saxon and Saxon," I mumbled, sucking the last bit of ice tea through my straw.

"Shit, Aria, that's a big deal."

I shrugged. I knew it was a big firm, but I wasn't going to make a huge fuss over it - especially when it was our connections that landed me the job.

I had majored in art history and creative writing - and I had no idea what to do next. Naturally, my parents stepped forward and landed me a job at a publishing house. It would be up to me to arrange book tours, signings, and all the fun bits in between.

"You're so full of it," Kerri waved a hand in my direction at my lack of reply.

I leant forward and grinned at her from across the table. "So, does this mean that tonight is our last night at O' Mally's until we all get back?"

She scrunched up her nose. "I suppose so," she grinned.

"I'll call Jack and tell him to book us a booth," she said, already lifting her phone to her ear.

Kerri and Jack had hooked up numerous times but refused to label their affair as anything more than friends with benefits. But I had seen the way Jack looked at Kerri across the bar when he thought no one was looking, and that was not the way you looked at a mere friend.

My last night of freedom. I swallowed audibly, my throat suddenly dry and constricting. I could get this back. I *would* get this back. I was trying to convince myself, willing it to be true.

But, the truth was that I didn't know how this experience would change me. I didn't know what would even be expected of me - because no one spoke about it. And I wasn't a complete idiot; The Society was definitely involved in some under-handed stuff, and I just wasn't sure how far they would drag me in, or even what those things were.

I shook myself out of my stupor, reminding myself that it was only three months, and that others got out. It was your *choice* around how involved you became. Besides, I had my job at Saxon and Saxon lined up, so there was no way that I would stay on past the time that was required of me.

"I'll meet you there at seven," I smiled across at her.

"Seven?" she queried. "That's pretty early, don't you think?"

"I want to make the most of our last night together," I shrugged it off, pushing the anxiety down that was threatening to swallow me.

"Sure, okay, is Nats coming?"

"Yeah," I answered on behalf of Natalia. "Count her in."

I stood up abruptly, aware of the time - aware that I needed to still pack my entire life into some luggage for three months *before* we hit O' Mally's tonight. Tomorrow, I would be handing myself over to The Society, but tonight was still *mine,* and I was going to hold it tight with both hands, taking everything it had to give.

"See you later," Kerri crooned, her hands glued to her phone as she texted Jack. I smiled knowingly, but did not say anything.

What did one even pack for three months with The Society? When I asked my mom, she simply told me to pack as if I were going on vacation, and that *they* - The Society - would provide anything else we needed.

This whole situation was so far removed from my reality that I didn't even know what to think of it. I had watched those conspiracy videos and honestly, it was easy to understand why The Society was vilified so much - for everything that we stood for, we still enjoyed our elitist hierarchy - *and* it was incredibly difficult to get in. In fact, most people married within The Society - settling down at a fairly young age because, honestly, how else would we be able to explain our "good fortune" to a significant other that wasn't in The Society.

Which is why what Natalia had was so very rare. She was dating a guy who was so far removed from our world. I didn't begrudge her for wanting to extend her time with him - taking an extra summer to forget what our families had obligated us to. But those pieces would undoubtedly crumble. The relationship would not last - because it would not be *allowed* to last. And so, I sat on the sidelines, watching my friend willingly barter her heart in a game that she was set to lose before it even began.

It was one of those whirlwind evenings that went past in a blur of laughter, spilled drinks, in-house jokes, ridiculous dancing and scream-singing along to the Slim Shady. I tried to *slow it down*. To hold those moments close. To be present and remember this night - what it felt like to be unencumbered by the world.

And when Natalia slipped away with Shawn, sneaking out the back door into the night, and Kerri slid beneath the bar, serving drinks side-by-side with Jack, I still danced, refusing to *let go*.

Shot after shot. I would be hungover for my first day with The Society, but I didn't care. My need to be in the here-and-now was simply too great. I needed to *live*. I needed to have some semblance of control over my own life; I needed to feel like I had a *choice*, because the truth is, I never really had a choice in how my life would play out, not really.

Shrugging off the bitterness of my thoughts, I drank another shot and felt a warm body slide next to me at the bar. I glanced over to see a red-headed boy flash me his classic smirk.

"Shots are the plan, huh?" He leant in, speaking close to my ear, his breath hitting my neck.

"Shut up, Mack, and drink with me." I slid a shot glass towards him.

"We are going to be fucked for tomorrow," he muttered before downing his drink.

I shrugged and continued drinking and dancing. I wasn't sure if I was still trying to live in the moment or simply forget what was expected of me.

Mack was from my world, and unsurprisingly, was giving his three months to The Society from tomorrow as well - right along with me. We knew each other, but not well. His friends were friends with my friends, but in a bid for independence, I tried not to make friends with too many Society kids. I wanted my life to be wholly my own. And, watching Mack down his shots, I wondered if he didn't feel the same.

CHAPTER TWO : THE ARRIVAL

The *thump thump thump* of my brain beat to the drum of my internal voice repeating, "I told you so."

Hungover, sitting upright and pert in the backseat of the black sedan that now drove through the steel structures of an estate, I wondered what exactly was in store for me.

The smell of my perfume caused a bout of nausea to rise up. I swallowed it down, annoyed at myself - and my body. I wondered how Mack was faring.

The Society boasted a few 'camps', scattered throughout the world. I just so happened to be stationed in a camp in Texas. One red eye flight and a car ride later and here I was, suffocating in the heat.

From the outside, the camp looked like a resort, and for the most part, I suppose it was. It boasted swimming pools, restaurants, coffee shops and some bars.

The building appeared foreboding in nature, or perhaps that was simply because I knew what it likely held - or rather, my imagination was running wild with those conspiracy theory possibilities.

My wedged Tommy Hilfiger shoes hit the neatly stoned area as the car stopped just outside the front doors of the lobby. Cool peach and copper tones decorated the entrance, giving one the illusion that this indeed was a hotel, and that you could, in fact, relax here.

That in itself put me on edge. My wariness crept in as I briefly wondered why they were trying to promote a relaxing atmosphere when they were The Society, and we were beholden to them - giving three months of our lives to them and their service.

The heat settled on me, suffocating in its nature, which only served to ensure that my head throbbed harder - if that was even possible.

I shifted my glasses neatly back up the bridge of my nose, lest anyone here think that I wasn't one hundred percent committed to this cause by not arriving as my best self.

From the outward appearance, I looked put together - or as my mother liked to emphasize, *impeccable*. Honestly, that dress sense had become second nature to me, and I shielded myself with the creation of an image.

Beige chinos, paired with a white-collared shirt, made me look like I was attending a business meeting, but it was the pearl necklace and earrings that offset it all, adding a touch of femininity to an otherwise largely masculine outfit.

As the glass doors slid open in a seemingly inviting fashion, I stepped into the world that had me questioning everything. The air-conditioned area skittered along my skin, leaving goosebumps in its wake. I shivered, wishing that I had a light jacket, despite the summer heat.

A woman stood in the center of the large marbled lobby area, clipboard in hand. Her dark hair was pulled back into a severe ballerina-style bun, pulling her facial features tight. She wore a dark black pantsuit, and everything about her spoke of authority.

She glanced up at me, giving me a tight-lipped smile, and suddenly, I wondered if I had somehow miss-stepped before I had even begun.

Who am I kidding? Of course I miss-stepped - I was hungover as a skunk.

"Aria O'Luc?" She spoke my name as if it were a question that she needed confirmation to, but we both knew that she knew exactly who I was. In fact, I had no doubt that that was what her job entailed.

I returned the smile, pushing my large sunglasses off my face into my hairline in a way that ensured my hair still framed my face well.

"That would be me," I confirmed.

Shit. Was that vodka I smelled wafting out from my pores?

I had never been one to regret my actions. In fact, I felt the act of regret and wallowing within the pool of self despair to be pretty redundant. Or - perhaps I had never committed an act that I was *truly* regretful for.

Steeling my spine, I waited for this woman to meet out her judgement. Her eyes flicked over my outfit in a way that was both condescending and patronising at the same time. As if I were a child in need of cuddling and handling.

Still, I suppressed my urge to rage at her and simply waited.

"You can go down the hallway and enter room C2 for orientation," she spoke, her eyes once more returned to her clipboard, as if I were no longer with her.

"Thank you," I uttered, my trained manners kicking in.

"Leave your luggage here, we will ensure that it is delivered to your room." She dismissed me without even looking up.

With little else left for me to do, I simply nodded my head, placing one foot in front of the other, marching down the hallway to see what lay in store for me.

Rows and rows of chairs facing towards a podium greeted me as I entered room C2. A few of the chairs were already occupied and I couldn't help but notice a shock of red hair sticking out from all ends as I spotted Mack, clad in a leather jacket. I wondered if he was as hungover as I was.

As if sensing me, he glanced over the back of his chair. Taking in my well put together outfit, he smirked. The bastard *knew* that I was hungover, and in the light of day, I fought the urge to flip him the finger.

I seated myself in the row behind Mack, towards the end, where I would have easy access should I need to... escape? I didn't even know what I was thinking.

Despite the chilled air-conditioned room, my palms were coated in sweat. I was nervous. Nauseatingly so. Or was that my hangover speaking?

I flicked through my phone, scrolling through social media apps as I watched my friends blast their summer plans across those platforms. My heart twisted a little, knowing what me being here meant - what I was giving up.

Because after this, I would know exactly what The Society was involved in - wouldn't I? I could no longer bury my head in the sand and ignore what wasn't being said. I would lose my naivety. So yes, a large part of me knew that I would be changed by this experience - and I honestly did not know if that change would be for the better.

I ignored the shuffling around me as the room filled up.

I just needed to get through this orientation, and then I could go and lie down and rest my pounding head. At least, that was the plan.

"Welcome," a voice boomed through the room, reverberating through me. I swallowed down the dryness in my throat, as I pushed down the panic that threatened to rise up.

This was happening. I was here. And I needed to get over myself and just get through these next few months.

I glanced over at Mack and saw his arm stretched across the back of the chair next to his - which just so happened to seat a petite blonde woman. Why was I not surprised?

But if Mack could take this in his stride, then so could I.

A hush descended upon the room as everyone settled in to listen to the broad male figure behind the podium.

He had greying hair, and fine wrinkles, but even from this distance I could see that he was well built beneath his suit.

"You are here today because your forefathers paved the foundation for this organisation." He spoke to the room. The silence in response was almost deafening.

No one responded. No one moved. No one dared to breathe too loudly.

"You are here today because it is *your* turn to ensure that we keep paving the way forward for *greatness*."

He remained silent for a beat, allowing his words to sink in.

"The world is adapting - changing and shifting all the time. But so are we - our society is mercurial by nature. The change in generations ensures that our ideas do not become stagnant - that we are able to forge forward with new ventures and creations on medicine, technology - and everything *the world* needs."

He took a sip of his water and continued.

"Many of you may not fully understand what we are about - as is the nature of our Society. The secretiveness, the want of your parents to *shield* you."

He paused dramatically.

"But," he said, "you are no longer children in need of shielding." He almost sneered the last word. "You are the next generation that will fan the flames of this organisation. You are the ones who will ensure that generations to come sit in this exact same spot in years to come. Greatness is created - it is not born, it is harvested, and that is what we will be doing here - harvesting for the future."

"Now," he raised his hand in an almost placating gesture. "Some of you will - *most* of you will not understand everything in one sitting, but by the end of these few months, I can promise that *all* of you will understand what we have achieved, and strive to continue to achieve. Those pillars of greatness will rest on *your* shoulders. Some of you will choose to remain working within our organisation, while others will take up positions around the globe, sowing the seeds of what we stand for in an array of different ways."

I swallowed down my confusion. The man had not told us *anything*. Not really.

"Now," he clapped, almost gleefully. "Some housekeeping. Sleeping quarters are always shared - we pair an experienced member of the organisation with an inexperienced member. This is to ensure that you truly immerse yourself in what we do here. It is too easy to stay within the bounds and friendship circles of comfort. I'm not an idiot." He chuckled at that, as if what he said was comical in itself. "I know a lot of you know one another. In our small circles, wielding the influence we do, it is impossible that most of you have never met - or are least know of each other. So, this pairing serves to render those boundaries useless. The only boundary in play is that of The Society."

The room broke out into applause, as if he had said something life changing.

"Now, now," he spoke over the thunderous noise. "We are also *very* fortunate to have some key instructors this season."

He cleared his throat, "Ajax SinClaire - my son - will once more be joining us, sharing and teaching his expertise in organisational takeovers."

A round of applause followed, with some of the crowd wolf whistling.

I watched a hand raise up from the front rows as a messy dark head of hair looked over his shoulder and smirked at the crowd.

Seems that Kerri was right - and that Ajax was definitely off the cards for her. He was a Society boy through and through.

"Next, I have to mention that we are very honoured to have General Paul Mae teaching combative skills -"

He was cut off as a row of girls began cheering as a bronzed man with a buzz cut - presumably Paul - stood up from the front row and took a mock bow.

"And," he pressed forward, laughing along at the interruption, "Military Strategist John Griffin teaching governmental organisation operations."

An older man with blonde hair, seated in the front row, simply raised his hand in response.

"And lastly, we have Sarah Lipson, who will be educating and training you on our humanity projects."

A small woman dressed in a navy skirt suit, with grayish-brown cropped hair, stood up from the front row and gave us all a small wave. She seemed almost harmless in nature.

"And I - Benson SinClaire - will be educating you on the history of The Society and all that we have managed to achieve."

He waved as the crowd clapped, despite it being unnecessary.

"You have the next two days to get settled, and then we will be commencing with our program. Now, I don't feel as if I should be telling you this, but I will anyway." His eyes scanned across the crowd, resting upon mine briefly before moving along.

A sense of unease rippled through me, but before I could truly examine it, he was talking once more.

"Have fun and be safe."

CHAPTER THREE : THE MIXER

As was apparently customary, The Society held a cocktail evening mixer for the summer attendees to get to know one another.

That was how I found myself standing at the bar in a floor length black dress, with thin spaghetti straps and a deep V open back.

I left my dark, long bob in waves, paired with a red lip. If the light caught my eyes *just right*, they would look amber, and not the dull brown I was accustomed to.

I knew I was beautiful. But when you are surrounded by wealth and influence, and are born into The Society, it is expected. In no way is it coveted, nor is it an achievement - it is simply expected.

I watched as a petite blonde woman that I had seen earlier sashayed towards the bar in a short, skin-tight, bright pink dress. My mother would be horrified. I was sure that she was a new recruit from one of the university societies - sometimes The Society found someone they thought was worth their time and offered them a spot within. It was rare, but not entirely unheard of.

And while beauty wasn't necessarily coveted - but rather expected amongst The Society - class was something my mother had instilled in me. I envied that blonde girl, abandoning caution and wearing what any party girl would. I envied her because my upbringing had never allowed for such things. But then - that was hardly a burden, was it?

A dark suit suddenly stood next to me, and once more I found myself standing next to Mack. His red hair stood out against his black jacket, his green eyes and high cheekbones twinkling in the light.

He grinned at me mischievously, "How is the hangover?"

I lifted the champagne glass to my lips, taking a deep sip before answering.

"Nothing some headache tablets and a nap couldn't cure," I finally answered, my eyes darting towards the blonde girl in the bright pink dress. She appeared slightly wobbly as she spun out onto the make-shift dance floor.

I narrowed my eyes in thought. Yes - that *was* the girl Mack had been sitting next to in Orientation.

"Looks like your date may need some assistance," I said.

"Oh yeah," Mack said, glancing back at her on the dance floor.

"Shit, I'll see you later," he muttered as he went to assist her.

Mack wasn't a bad guy. I supposed none of them were here. Or if they did like to prey on drunk women, no one would see it here simply because *everyone* who was an attendee was related to someone of importance. Wasn't that the sad truth.

I wandered around aimlessly, champagne flute clenched between my fingers as I took it all in. The vibrancy on the dance floor. The cigar smoke wafting out from the bar. I watched in amusement as a flash of dark hair was dragged into the bathrooms by a girl in a blue dress.

Without evening meaning to, I stepped out onto the large terraced balcony. The warmth of the night settled upon my skin, relaxing me in a way that reminded me exactly how tense I had been since I arrived.

I felt him before I saw him. His presence domineering and all masculine. He leant against the railing next to me as I stared down at the pool below, the lights within the water beckoning.

I heard him exhale loudly, but still I didn't say anything, nor did I move. I simply stood next to this stranger.

We remained in silence for a long time - touching, but not really touching either.

He was the first to break the silence.

"Have you met your roommate yet?" His voice was low and scratchy, as if he had smoked a full box of Texan plains.

I glanced up at him and realised that it was General Paul Mae that had squeezed himself next to me. I was so much smaller than him.

Blue eyes shone out from a handsome face filled with humour. And in this close proximity, I saw that his hair was a light brown.

"No," I laughed out. "Why do you ask?"

He remained quiet for a second too long.

"What?" I glanced up at him.

He grimaced.

"Nothing." he shook his head, suddenly trailing a finger up my spine.

I shivered at the contact.

"You look so damn unattainable." He shivered into my neck, sending a pool of warmth straight to my core.

I heard a commotion behind me and turned to find Ajax and another dark-haired man tumbling through the balcony doors.

"That's it," the dark-haired man (whose name I did not know yet) spoke, "time is up," he announced.

I watched as Paul grimaced, and before I could ask what was going on, the stranger continued. "We gave you thirty minutes to hook up or get the fuck out - and do you know what you did with that time?"

Heat flooded my face. I was simply part of their stupid game of hookup.

"You stared at the fucking swimming pool," the stranger continued.

I glanced up to find Paul smiling at me regretfully, giving me a light shrug in response to those unsaid things.

"Excuse me," I said, stepping around them as I re-entered the mixer.

I felt three sets of eyes follow me as I walked towards the bar. And fuck it if I did not arch my back *slightly*, sway my hips just a little bit more than necessary. I refused to be embarrassed. And I refused to be part of their game.

It was as if this reprieve from the real world had everyone acting on base instincts, as if they were frat boys.

I caught Mack's eye as he helped his date along towards the exit. I gave him a small smile whilst he dipped his head in acknowledgement.

At the end of the day, it was up to me whether I chose to play or not. And because I already wasn't sure what I had signed up for in these three months, I felt far safer *not* playing.

On the opposite side of the bar, I noticed a card game being dealt. I made my way over, noticing an empty seat, and made myself comfortable.

A beautiful woman with whisky coloured hair and green-grey eyes smiled wickedly at me.

"You in?" She nodded at me, dealing for the two men opposite her, as well as herself.

"Yes," I nodded.

A pile of cards landed in front of me as the game was in play.

I learnt that the two men opposite me had both given The Society their three months of time last summer, but they had returned to work ad hoc on the humanities projects.

The woman's name was Raquel - and she simply oozed sex appeal.

"This your first time?" She asked, referencing my three-month time period.

"And last," I nodded.

She laughed. "They all say that. Don't be so sure until you've taken the whole ride - then decide." She winked at me.

A new hand of cards was dealt. And another. And another. That is how I spent most of the evening - and I did not hate it.

"You're Nats' friend, right?" Raquel asked.

I stared up in surprise.

"She told me to look out for you," she laughed out once more. "Her parents and my parents are… friends".

"Friends?"

She shrugged. "We actually think that they're swingers, but we have no proof. So yes - friends."

I coughed slightly as my drink slid down my throat.

Raquel actually laughed.

"You're too easy to mess with," she shrugged.

"I hate you," I muttered - a smile tugging at my lips.

"No, you don't," she grinned. "I'm going to be your best fucking friend here."

And just like that, I knew that I liked her. And maybe - if I came out of this experience with a friendship, it wouldn't be all bad.

We played a few more rounds before I folded and retreated for the night.

My suite looked exactly the same as when I had left it - which meant that my roommate still had not been here. Maybe I lucked out and simply did not have a roommate?

The suite consisted of two bedrooms - the master bedroom with an ensuite bathroom and large double bed sprawled in the middle of the room, and the second room with a small single bed pressed up against the wall. The living area is a largely open plan with a kitchenette, small dining area and a couch positioned in front of a TV.

Naturally, I took the master bedroom - because honestly, why wouldn't I?

I undressed and slid beneath the covers, eager to sleep in. I had one more day of this before the programme commenced. Maybe I would even take a swim? The sound of laughter from the swimming pool drifted through the window, but I honestly did not care. I had two messages that I still needed to reply to - one from Nats and one from my mother. *Tomorrow*. I would reply to them *tomorrow*. For now, I just wanted to sleep.

I sank deeper into the mattress as I willed my body to relax, and soon enough, sleep engulfed me, claiming me with the vengeance that was exhaustion.

Somewhere from the depths of sleep, I heard the sound of the front door of the suite open and close. Some shuffling, followed by a loud thud. I heard the water running from the second bathroom, followed by a deep sigh.

It seemed my roommate had finally arrived. I closed my eyes and allowed sleep to drag me under. *Tomorrow*. I would meet her tomorrow.

I felt the mattress dip next to me and instinctually bolted upright. Leaning across the bed, I switched on the light, ready to tell my roommate off.

"The fuck?" A very masculine voice answered groggily.

Ajax SinClaire was lying in his boxer shorts on the bed. Aware of my state of undress, I pulled the sheet higher up, making sure that I was covered. By the looks of it, it did not even matter. He was so drunk and out of it, I would be surprised if he knew his own name.

"What are you doing in my room?" I ground out.

And for a moment, Ajax opened his eyes and seemed genuinely confused to see me there.

"I swear, if this is another one of your games of *hookup*, it's not going to work," I huffed.

He blinked, as if trying to clear the haze.

"This is my room," he said in a way that booked no argument.

"No," I ground out, "this is my room."

We stared at each other until I felt the need to further emphasise my point.

"Unless you're my *roommate*, you don't get to stay in this suite. And this," I pointed to the bed, "is *my* room."

Ajax threw his head back and laughed. There had to be something wrong with him. He was drunk. That's what was wrong with him. He had obviously stumbled into the wrong room, and *that* was the joke.

I loosened my frown a little, relieved to be making sense of all of this.

"Darling," he spluttered, "*I* am your roommate."

I stared at him. This wasn't possible. Wasn't I supposed to have a girl as a roommate? How could I be so naive?

I cleared my throat, trying to regain some semblance of order.

"Fine," I narrowed my eyes, "then go to *your* room."

He stopped laughing and returned my glare.

"*This* is my room," he said.

"No," I shook my head out, "when I arrived here, this place was entirely empty, and as you can see, *I* have now occupied it."

He stared at me.

"Go on," I pointed towards the door, "go to your room."

He narrowed his gaze.

"That room is shit and has a single bed, and darling - I'm a big man, so why don't you take your petite, pretty self and slip into the small bed and leave me here?"

I couldn't help it. I spluttered a laugh.

"Did you actually think that was going to work?"

He pouted and if I did not find him so infuriating, I may have found that adorable.

He finally looked at me with more clarity than before.

"Are you naked?" He asked incredulously.

I glanced down to make sure the sheet was still in place, knowing that my face was burning up.

"Get. Out!" I hissed.

He laughed, retreating to the doorway. Before leaving entirely, he said, "I'm serious about the bed thing though - we can talk about it in the morning - maybe do a rotation of who gets the big bed - "

"Out!" I interrupted him

I shrugged, and he lopped off into the darkness.

Tomorrow. I would deal with it all tomorrow, I tried to convince myself as I sunk back down into the pillows once more.

CHAPTER FOUR : IT'S ALL ABOUT PERCEPTION

As the sun filtered through the window, glaring across the room, I woke up reluctantly.

It was not a watery, easy kind of sunlight. Rather, it was bright, demanding and as unrelenting as Texas itself.

I did not tip-toe through the suite, nor did I go about getting ready quietly. In fact, I *may have* been slightly louder than necessary.

I knew Ajax would be sporting a pounding headache in all his hungover glory, but I did not give a flying fig - especially when he wanted to lay claim to my bed.

Asshole.

I decided that I would treat this experience as a vacation - well, as much of it as I could. And so, in that fashion, I chose to have my breakfast at one of the outdoor restaurants overlooking the pool, and then my plans for the day largely revolved around lounging by said pool, swimming, possibly reading my book and scrolling my phone.

Call me an old person, but after nearly being caught up in Paul's game of *hookup*, I felt as if playing it safe was probably best.

The loungers were neatly positioned around the pool, a large overhanging umbrella positioned between two.

I picked at my breakfast as nausea rolled through me. I was actually here - in The Society. I watched as people slowly started emerging from their suites, splashing and playing in the pool. A game of volleyball ensued, and I wondered why I couldn't let this ominous feeling go and just enjoy my time here. Why was I always so damn skeptical?

Nats: this is so much more difficult than I thought it would be. I have no idea how I'm going to end things with him at the end of summer.

I reread the message, not really knowing what I should say or what support I could offer.

Sighing, I moved on to the message from my mother, deciding that I would return to Nat's message when I actually knew what to say.

Mom: How did orientation go? What did you wear to the mixer? Please, just be careful and safe while you're there.

I rolled my eyes at my mother's message. She was referring to sex. But she would never come out and say that - because that would be 'unladylike'. I snorted. It seems that my mother wasn't entirely oblivious to what occurred in this compound.

"Wanna tell me what that smirk is all about?"

I glanced up, startled by Raquel's intrusion.

She sank into the lounger next to me, stretching out as though she were a cat baking in the sunshine.

"You know, you need to take your cover-up off if you plan on getting any kind of tan," she continued, without missing a beat.

I huffed out a laugh as I realised that I had been so caught up with my internal dialogue that I was still sitting on the lounger dressed in a cover-up and shorts.

I slid the black shift off my shoulders and kicked off my shorts, revealing a cherry red bikini.

"Well, if the guys were not looking at us before, they certainly are now," Raquel muttered.

"What?" I defended/ "It's not like no one else is here in a bikini!"

I squinted at her and shrieked, "see - you're even wearing one!" I exclaimed.

Raquel was wearing a dark blue bikini that - judging from the side view I was getting - was a high cut thong.

"One," she lifted a finger, "mine is not *siren* red, and two - no one else looks like *you*."

"What does that mean?" I huffed.

She squinted at me.

"Seriously? You can't be that fucking oblivious."

I continued to stare at her, waiting for her to expand upon her statement.

"You look like a goddamn runway model," she exclaimed, exasperated.

I began denying it, but Raquel interrupted me, "If you try and tell me you're *not* pretty, I'm going to assume that you're stupid and will no longer continue this friendship."

"Everyone in The Society is beautiful. It's as if they systematically bred everyone that way," I defended.

"And yet," she raised a glass of - what looked like orange juice - in my direction and continued, "none of them look like *you."*

"We're going to have to agree to *disagree*," I replied curtly.

"Right," Raquel responded sarcastically.

We lay there in the sun, people watching.

Mack spotted me from across the pool and waved. I waved back.

"You two a thing?" Raquel asked.

"Not in the least, we just went to the same university."

A comfortable silence engulfed us as I scrolled through apps on my phone. A human sized shadow blocked my sun, causing me to look up.

"Hello, Darling," Ajax stood over me.

"Oh look, he lives."

"You wound me," he clutched his chest, and I rolled my eyes.

"What do you want?"

"We need to discuss the bed situation," he said with a deadpan expression.

Raquel snickered from beside me. I cut her a glare.

"There is nothing to discuss," I said smoothly, "now move - you're in my sun."

"Stop being such a primadonna and be reasonable," he ground out, fists clenching at his sides.

"How's the headache?" I responded sweetly.

"You are incorrigible."

"I've been called worse," I said, looking back at my phone.

"Can you not see that you are much smaller than me and therefore *should* take the smaller bed?" He demanded.

I heard Raquel grumble something about sharing her bed, but couldn't quite make out the exact wording.

"And this is why I won't even entertain the idea. The fact that you are so arrogant - so sure that the master bedroom is your *right,* is infuriating. So NO, I will not simply switch rooms with you-"

He started to interrupt, but I ploughed forward, "- nor will we do a 'bed rotation' - this is not a custody battle. If you don't like your living quarters, then take it up with management. I'm sure they would be happy to find you new accommodations."

He stood silent, the muscle in his jaw pulsing. "What's wrong?" I goaded, "You can't find someone else's bed to slide into?"

He jerked back, as if the insult made physical contact with him.

"You're such a bitch," he seethed.

"Yeah, imagine my delight when I got paired up with you. The asshole who was participating in a childish game of *hookup* last night. Maybe if you weren't such an adolescent, you would have been able to claim the room sooner because you would have actually been there, but as it stands, the master suite is mine."

Raquel snickered once more.

"It's a good thing you're so beautiful because you have *nothing* else going for you - your personality and character are absolutely dog shit."

I laid back lazily and replied, "at least I have a personality."

He stalked off as I called after him in a sing-song voice, "good luck finding another bed".

Once he was out of earshot, Raquel turned to me and laughed outright, "Your roommate is Ajax SinClaire!"

"Don't remind me," I grumbled.

"I can't wait to see how this plays out," she gushed.

"You mean, if he'll find another bed?" I scrunched my nose up as I said, "I'm sure some woman here will accommodate him."

"No, I mean that I don't think anyone has really challenged Ajax before because well, he's *Ajax, and* his dad runs this place - kind of, but you just had a throw down with him - over a bed - don't think people aren't going to be talking about this."

I glanced across the pool and realised that people were, in fact, looking at us, and suddenly, I felt as if I were in high school all over again, with all my insecurities rising once more to the surface.

"I'm guessing it won't be the first, or the last time, that people discuss where Ajax is sleeping," I replied, and we both burst into a fit of giggles at that.

I don't know why Ajax being part of The Society surprised me - perhaps because Kerri was set to work for his company, but I supposed it all fit - he was a Society kid just like me. Actually, he was worse because his father was so involved with their operations. He probably wasn't shielded as I was growing up, and it seemed he embraced this lifestyle fully. I pushed down the niggly feeling that tended to rise up everytime I thought about how The Society operates - because in truth; I did not know how they operated and so my feelings did not make sense. Perhaps research bias, based on the conspiracy theories I had read?

As I stood up to swim, I watched as some people gazed at me, taking in my exposed figure in all its glory. From this distance, I could see Ajax seated at the pool bar, his back towards me. He was flanked by Paul and the mystery man from last night. One of them must have said something to him because he swivelled in his chair, looking over his shoulder to glare at me. I dipped my head and smiled in acknowledgement. Two could play this game.

Raquel convinced me to go another round of poker - arguing that we needed to make a standard poker night once a week while we were here, because if guys could do it then why the hell couldn't we?

I bemoaned the fact that Raquel wasn't my roommate, and that I was stuck with Ajax. Perhaps his father would pull some strings and move him, I thought hopefully.

The day bled into the night with food, drinks, and good company. Raquel was actually a lot of fun and seemed to be game for anything. Our poker night attracted the same guys as the night before - I learnt that their names were Rob and Lyle. Mack also joined, a smirk always present on his face.

"I heard you ruffled some feathers, O'Luc?" He said, dragging out my surname.

"Don't even get me started," I responded, only to be met with a volley of laughter.

He raised his hand in surrender. "Don't shoot the messenger for the talk that's doing the rounds."

"Oh?" I asked, raising an eyebrow, "and what talk might that be?"

I watched his Adam's apple bob as he swallowed, and I could not tell if he was nervous or excited.

His trademark smirk soon replaced that uncertainty as he said, "that you don't want Ajax in your bed."

Raquel joined Rob and Lyle as they laughed outright once more.

"Of course, that's what is being said. Of course, that's what people have taken out of what happened," I groaned, clutching my head.

Mack simply shook his head and chose to continue staring at his hand of cards. In the end, he ended up winning, cleaning us all out, looking as if he were the cat who ate the cream.

That night, as I entered the suite, there was no sign of Ajax, and for that I was grateful. Careful not to be found naked again, I slid into a silk slip and lay in bed, willing my overactive thoughts to dissipate.

CHAPTER FIVE : SWIPE RIGHT

By the time morning rolled around, I still had seen no sign of Ajax SinClaire - which suited me just fine.

We had all received a timetable, of sorts, covering the different time slots and corresponding lectures. Large blocks had been blanked out for 'assignments', and I could only imagine what that was.

I was in summer school - that's what this was. All those good grades seemed to have been for naught. I sighed, resigning myself to a day of lectures

My first taste of what The Society was truly about was in governmental organisation operations, taught by military Strategist John Griffin.

A glass screen stood in place of the typical blackboard. Rows and rows of chairs were spread across the room, each row raised slightly higher than the previous one.

The small auditorium was impressive, not simply because of its aesthetic appeal, but largely due to the small hints of luxury it exposed.

The seats were a soft caramel leather, with each chair containing a small desk tray that could be unfolded and positioned at will.

I sank into the leather, and despite the softness of the seat, the coolness of the leather itself bit at me, reminding me that I couldn't relax here. I held onto that feeling, lest I become complacent.

Control. Control. Control.

That is what this class pretty much came down to. How governments control people, land, agriculture, medicine, technology and structural development.

I felt in even less control of my life than I had before I arrived here.

No one took notes - it wasn't that kind of class, in fact it was more of an eye-opener kind of class. They were laying the foundation of why The Society was necessary, and while I had little doubt that it may have begun with altruistic motives, it certainly had not maintained that same momentum.

To make matters worse, John Griffin was boring as all hell. He may have been an amazing Military Strategist, but make no mistake, no one was cozying up around the fire with him because of his story-telling abilities.

Mack was positioned a few seats down from me, his head resting on the table.

"Looks like you have a little drool there," I teased, pointing at his mouth once the class had finished and we were all shuffling out. He jerked awake as I walked past him.

"Shut up, O'Luc," he grumbled.

We bottlenecked at the doorway, Mack squeezed against me.

"Why didn't we ever hang out at uni?" He asked as we waited.

I suppressed my grimace, lest he think it was because of who he is and not simply that he was a Society kid.

"I just wanted to forget about this whole thing for a bit, I guess," I shrugged.

"And you thought by not hanging out with other Society members, but still attending one of the most prestigious universities in the country, that that would happen?"

I laughed at the absurdity of hearing it aloud.

He shook his head, joining me in laughter.

Directly in front of us were two girls, whispering and giggling with one another, and I felt a pang in my chest as I realised how much I missed Nat, and what was worse is that I did not even *think* I would miss her this much.

"... so are you saying you didn't sleep with him?" The dark-haired woman in front of me asked the gorgeous auburn-haired girl.

Her muffled giggle carried towards us, causing Mack to crease his brow. I shot him a questioning look. He just shook his head in a silent response.

And so we stood behind them in silence, serving as unwilling eavesdroppers.

"So," the auburn-haired beauty hushed her voice even further, "he was crazy adamant that he wouldn't have *sex* with me, *but* he made up for in other ways…"

The dark-haired girl elbowed her for more information.

"Okay, fine," she laughed out, "he may or may not have… exercised his *tongue* muscle, excessively."

Once more, they both burst into a fit of laughter.

"Okay, so was it good?" The dark-haired woman asked.

I rolled my eyes so hard I'm surprised no one else in the room felt it. What a typical question.

She giggled once more, "Let's just say that I have an open door policy for him to visit me *anytime.*"

They sniggered together once more, and I had to remind myself that they were doing nothing wrong, and that if Nats had been here, we would probably be doing the same thing.

"Yeah, but he kept asking if I was sure that he could spend the night in my bed," she scrunched up her face in confusion and added, "as if I were going to kick him out".

"Believe me," the woman with dark hair interjected, "no woman in their right mind would kick Ajax out of their bed."

And just like that, my eavesdropper interest cooled, leaving the taste of distrust in my mouth.

As the bottleneck eased through the doorway, I mentally shut myself off from their conversation. I did not need to hear about Ajax's sexual activities in any way or form.

The cafeteria was buzzing with static as everyone seemed to tumble out of their morning lectures. Mack was still stuck by my side, which was surprising in itself. It wasn't as if he and I were friends, not really.

While the purpose of the cafeteria was essentially to keep us all fed, it did not look like a typical cafeteria, rather it looked like a restaurant that had been entombed in greenery.

Potted plants hung from the ceiling sporadically, some low enough that you were forced to duck your head to avoid injury. Vines crept along the opposite interior wall.

Wrought-iron tables curled and flowed across the floor, the brick paving beneath creating grooves and edges in its wake.

A large open triangular shaped skylight sat in the centre of the ceiling, casting shafts of sunlight down upon us. The sound of flowing water was soothing and relaxing, reminding me of simpler - or perhaps more ignorant - times. And right there, nestled between the creeping ivy on the wall, was a water feature depicting angels and devil's dancing as water flowed from their mouth into the catching fountain dish below, only for that same water to be pumped back up for the process to be repeated once more. Images of children fainting between them were evident, but the children did not have water flowing from their mouths. It seemed like a personal torment for these characters, the forced need to regurgitate the same thing time and time again, whilst being in forced proximity with their supposed enemies.

Wordlessly, Mack and I sat at one of the tables closest to the ivy wall, and we were soon joined by Raquel, Rob and Lyle. Somewhere in the past few days we had cemented a friendship, and it looked like it was sticking past orientation.

Raquel sat down with a smirk plastered on her face.

"What?" I asked her from across the table as two waiters placed dishes in front of each of us.

My question seemed to have detonated something at the table because they all packed out, laughing.

"Seriously?" I asked, indigent.

Mack shook his head, wrangling his laughter under control.

"He slept in another woman's bed and didn't even have sex with her to get away from *you*," he said.

I groaned, sinking my face into my hands.

"How does everyone know?" I groaned into my palms.

"Because," Raquel chimed in, "the girl he was with has been praising his… *talents* the whole morning."

I glanced up to glare at her.

"We *just* walked out of our morning lecture - how is it even possible that *everyone* knows already?"

"You missed the breakfast rush, but that girl was bragging about 'Ajax SinClaire' sleeping in her bed." Raquel, once again, offered her insight, a grin plastered across her face.

"You're enjoying this too much," I grumbled.

"Absolutely," she agreed, "you have no idea how *boring* last summer was."

I felt people glance in our direction - looking at the girl, who had somehow ensured that Ajax did not have a place to sleep. In response, I steeled my spine, sat taller, and stabbed my salad with deliberate precision. I knew that the rumour mill would spin, fabricating the story that I had somehow rejected Ajax, refusing him admittance into *my* bed. And I did not give a flying fig.

My jeans suddenly felt too tight - too restrictive, as if I were somehow gearing up for a fight and needed all my limbs to move with ease.

As expected, Ajax walked through the cafeteria and seated himself towards the center. Paul, and the dark-haired man that always seemed to be with them, joined him.

"Who is the other guy?" I caved, asking Raquel.

Emotion flickered in her eyes - too quickly for me to determine exactly what it was.

"That," she spoke with a forced smile, "Is Joshua Penn."

I blinked, trying to decipher if that information meant something to me - or rather, if it *should* have meant something to me.

"He grew up with Ajax, and his family were the *founders* of Penn University," Raquel huffed out.

Oh. *Oh*. Shit, I should have actually known that.

"So, what is he doing here?" I asked nonchalantly.

"What we're all doing here," Mack chimed in, "paying our dues."

It seemed as if I wasn't the only one resentful of the system.

It wasn't that I wasn't grateful for the opportunities that were served up on a silver platter; it was that I did not have a choice in whether I *wanted* those opportunities or not.

"What do you have after lunch?" Mack asked me.

"Organisational take-overs," I grimaced in reply.

CHAPTER SIX : DISTANCE

The auditorium that I found myself in was a copy and paste replica of the previous one. The only difference was that it was Ajax SinClaire, who stood beside the podium, welcoming everyone to his class.

I wish I could say that he was rude and obnoxious to me because I had somehow 'shunned' him in all his glory by not handing over my bed, but the truth was, he ignored me completely.

As his eyes grazed over the room, they hovered over me for a millisecond, and then simply moved on. Mack chuckled next to me, which told me that it did not go completely unnoticed.

Ajax's lecture centred on the need for The Society to infiltrate and take over corporations and organisations. I grew to understand that The Society controlled all the pharmaceutical companies, with their belief sitting on the ability and need to prevent any truly disastrous medicinal rollouts.

"And let's not kid ourselves," Ajax said to the room, "the money within the pharmaceutical industry is pretty good."

A few women seated in the front row giggled in response and I had to use all my self-control to *not* dry heave.

Something about what he was saying did not sit right. I mean - why were the pharmaceutical companies always at war with one another if they were all essentially owned by The Society?

I raised my hand in the air, my shirt pulling tightly, and watched Ajax grimace when he saw me.

Asshole.

"Yes, Aria?"

Looks like he knew my name.

"Why are the pharmaceutical companies continually competing and bidding against one another? Surely, if The Society owns them, it would be smarter to share those resources between the firms, rather than compete?"

"One," he raised a finger in the air, "they do share resources - that is how they have been able to supply medicines in such a timeous manner to the Globe, and two," he lifted a second finger up, "we make *more* money through giving the illusion of competition as it often drives the prices up in a way that is market-related and acceptable *and* through hosting competing companies, the public would never assume that we control them all - because much like you, Miss O'Luc, they would assume that the companies would share information in lieu of competing, but as you can see, it is not an either or circumstance."

I felt my face growing flush with embarrassment as Ajax SinClaire highlighted my 'short-sightedness' in front of a full auditorium.

I heard the snickers from the audience, but refused to give them my attention.

Unable to sit there stone-faced, I pushed forward, "So, The Society would rather make the highest profit off of *medicines* rather than offering the world a glimpse of non-competing pharmaceutical companies working side-by-side and creating the *same* medicines, simply at a fraction of the cost? The Society could actually save more people."

Ajax's gaze narrowed upon me. "Oh excuse me, I did not realise that you were a bleeding heart. You did not seem to question these ethics when you attended your elite university, or when you went on your shopping expeditions - and, my goodness Miss O'Luc," he spoke in mock horror, "is that a *Burberry* shirt that you are wearing?"

He dismissed me with a flick of his eyes and addressed the entire auditorium. "The Society has ensured that the globe and its populace have remained safe throughout history. We have been at the grassroots of economic development and job creation. We have teams and teams of people who work tirelessly for an array of *humanity* projects that combat all the ugliness of this world. But," he paused dramatically, "those projects require funding, and our pharmaceutical enterprises fund a lot of the good that we are able to do."

The auditorium broke out into a buzz as people began to chatter. Ajax raised his hand, halting the talk, and ploughed forward with his speech.

"Now, that isn't to say that if someone is truly in dire need and requires these medicines but cannot afford them, that we won't - and don't - help. In fact, we have a number of NGO projects and community health-clinic run programmes that give those in financial difficulty access to what they need - although there may be some administrative tasks those individuals are required to complete, the assistance is, and always will, be there."

The crowd seemed to settle down somewhat, with two of the women in the front row looking back at me to shoot me nasty looks.

The blonde girl who had been with Mack at orientation sat two rows ahead of us and raised her own hand.

"Yes, Marissa." Ajax answered her.

"So, if The Society essentially owns all the pharmaceutical companies, does that mean that they are responsible for our birth control?"

I watched in fascination as Ajax's muscle in his jaw tightened, ticking in agitation.

"Yes," he said, "I suppose that they are responsible for your birth control, seeing as they create it."

Marissa nodded and continued, "But do they specifically monitor The Society individuals' medication and birth control?"

It was Ajax's turn to nod his head in understanding, "Yes, they have everyone's health records on file for medical purposes."

Her brow creased in confusion, and before she could ask another question, Ajax thanked us all for attending and dismissed us.

Mack and I shuffled our way towards the door, and I noticed that the auburn-haired beauty from early was lingering at the podium.

"Hey, Jessica." Ajax greeted her with a bland smile - and even I could tell that it didn't look promising.

Her face brightened at the mention of her name.

"I was thinking that tonight -"

He cut her off before she could say anything further. "Jess, you seem like a nice enough girl, but I like to keep my nose clean, so I don't really date Society girls."

Her face flushed crimson.

Asshole.

"Well, I don't think last night had *anything* to do with *dating*, but fine."

"Glad we're on the same page," he replied.

Because of the bottleneck at the door (once again), a lot of people overheard Jessica's dismissal. Worse yet, she couldn't even flee the situation and was stuck lingering behind us whilst Ajax neatly stacked his paperwork together.

"Drinks at Joe's?" Mack asked.

"Yeah," I replied quietly, appalled at Ajax.

After finally emerging from the auditorium, Jessica shouldered past me, fleeing down the hallway. I didn't envy her one bit.

The permanent fog that was cigar smoke clouded the interior of Joe's. It was one of two bars on the premises, but somehow Joe's didn't feel quite as done up as the other one. It had faded green carpets and an old stage that hosted karaoke. The wooden bar looked as if it had seen better days, and I felt more at home here than I did in any other part of the compound.

Raquel was already there, a bottle of champagne seated on the table.

"What's this?" I grinned at her.

"What?" she asked innocently. "You and Mack survived your first day of 'class' here."

"And you?" I asked.

"I'm here for round two, baby."

"You wouldn't be celebrating if you saw how Ajax and her interacted in his class?" Mack added.

"Did he flirt with you?" Raquel asked, gobsmacked.

"No," I ground out.

"He can't stand her," Mack contributed helpfully.

I shrugged as if it didn't bother me, but the truth was that I quite liked being liked, and I wasn't accustomed to such open hostility. I suppose it was due to my gilded cage and the doors my family name opened.

"Speaking of class," I quickly changed the topic, "what was up with Marissa's questions today?"

Mack pressed his lips in a thin line before answering, "She was trying to get Ajax to admit that The Society has a breeding programme."

I sat in shocked silence, but Mack continued, oblivious to the ground that had been pulled out from under me.

"I told her it was stupid - I *told her* not to bring it up, so that was her roundabout way of asking."

He finally looked at me, and the panic on my face must have been evident.

"You didn't know?" He raised his eyebrows, his tone one of disbelief.

"Aria - how can you not know?" Raquel chimed in.

I shrugged my shoulders in response.

"How fucking sheltered did your parents keep you?" Mack demanded.

My heart ached at the betrayal. There was 'sheltered' and then there was betrayal - they knew that I would be walking in here blind. How could they do that? Why hadn't my mother prepared me?

"Apparently, *very.*" I croaked.

It was Mack and Raquel's turn to sit in silence, until I eventually said, "Are either of you going to tell me about the breeding programme?"

Mack and Raquel seemed to have a silent conversation with one another before Mack cleared his throat. "So you know how people within The Society tend to only procreate with other members in The Society?"

"Yeah?" I said in confusion. "I thought that was like a non-written rule - you *have* to settle down with someone in The Society."

Mack nodded in relief, pleased to see that I wasn't entirely in the dark.

"Okay, but because we're a pretty exclusive group, The Society usually keeps a curated list of *who* you can hook up with - and who you can't because they don't really want us knocking out kids with a third cousin or some shit."

"But it's more than that," Raquel interjected, "the list also highlights characteristics and traits to ensure the best possible *breeding* outcome."

I squinted in confusion. "So, are you saying that there are only a handful of people I would even be *allowed* to settle down with?"

They both nodded.

"Because our mixed traits would produce the best offspring - that would essentially belong to The Society."

Raquel bit her lip nervously and nodded.

I closed my eyes briefly and asked, "So, that's why she was asking about birth control - because once The Society gives you the green light on your relationship, they take you off birth control?"

Mack cleared his throat once more. "It is expected that the couple produce at least one child for The Society."

"Wait," I shook my head, "but some Society parents have more than one child."

Mack shrugged. "One can only assume that those are *happy* relationships, where they actually *wanted* to have kids with each other."

I blinked.

"What are you saying?" My eyebrows drew down in a mix of confusion and anger.

"That at the end of the day, you get a choice of a handful of people that you need 'settle down' with - and if you don't choose, then The Society will make the choice for you. Often it's not love - or even lust, but rather an expected *arrangement*," he spat.

I closed my eyes at the onslaught of emotions.

"But I'm an only child," I whispered.

"Most here are," Mack replied, the muscles in his neck tense.

I excused myself and left. I needed time to process this information.

The Society had a breeding programme? It was going to be a type of arrangement. I wouldn't get a choice in who I would marry - in who I would have children with. I was such an idiot - I had been so naive in assuming I had *any* control over my life - any control over *this*.

I briefly wondered who was on my list.

And I was an only child. Did that mean that my parents were forced into this marriage? They were forced to have me? How my mother didn't resent me, I didn't know. Did they love each other? Like each other?

I pressed my palms against my eyelids in a bid to stem the flow of tears that were now trickling down my face.

I was the result of the best mix of genes between these two people in The Society - nothing more, nothing less. And when it came time for me to work in my servitude, my parents happily gave me up - because that was what was expected of them.

I always sort of *knew* that my parents didn't have a loving relationship, but on some level I believed that something had shifted and changed along the way - not that it had been like that from the beginning.

I wondered how clinical this entire process was. Was there a box that I ticked saying yes to one person and no to another? Who's list was I on? And once we decided it was simply a clerical and administrative matter, whereby The Society would orchestrate the marriage. Of course, with our families and connections, it didn't matter who I married, the wedding itself would be a production.

I sat cross-legged on my bed, the waves of grief ebbing and flowing as my crying took a stop-start approach. I was mourning the loss of my freedom. I was mourning the perceived control I had over my life. I was mourning the fact that parents were not honest with me. And I was mostly mourning because there was a very real possibility that somewhere along the line, I would be forced to enter into an arranged, loveless marriage.

The level of control The Society exerted over us was frightening, and I swallowed down my questions about them once more.

My head throbbing from all the tears I had spent, I fell back onto the pillows and simply lay there.

I heard the front door of the suite open and close suddenly. My body went rigid and I sat up as my bedroom door flung open.

Ajax stood in the doorway looking at me. "Ah fuck," he muttered, looking at my red-splotchy face - I knew it wasn't a pretty sight, and I could not find it in me to care.

"I came to talk about our living arrangements," he spoke stagnantly, "but I can't talk to you like *this*."

I watched him, unable - and unwilling - to offer an explanation. He *knew*. He knew about the breeding programme - it was why he had avoided Marissa's questions today.

"You knew about the breeding programme," I croaked, my voice hoarse from crying. I swallowed down my shame at feeling weak and vulnerable.

His face registered his surprise before he once more schooled his face into a blank expression.

"Everyone knows," he said, his voice void of emotion.

"We'll talk about our living arrangements in the morning," he said, turning away from my door.

I collapsed back onto the bed, waiting for sleep to engulf me. Perhaps I would find peace within the darkness.

CHAPTER SEVEN : THE ARRANGEMENT

My head felt groggy as I woke up, and while I was feeling more in control of my emotions, I was also still incredibly sad. I got dressed mechanically. Years of practiced work instilled by my mother had me emerging from my room looking more presentable.

I opted for a cherry red playsuit with a sweetheart neckline, pairing it with my leather jacket. And although it was ridiculous, the act of sliding the leather jacket across my shoulders made me feel *braver* somehow - as if I could actually accomplish all the things I wanted in life.

My phone vibrated softly as a message from Nats came through.

Nat: Thinking of you!

She had attached a picture of the little coffee shop we went to in Greece, and suddenly I knew that she didn't know the truth either, because if she did she would be running away with Paul, not simply having a last vacation with him.

Sliding my phone back into my bag, I stepped over the threshold of my room into the open plan living area where I found Ajax seated at the kitchen counter, a jug of coffee positioned on the table with two mugs set down.

I raised my brow skeptically at him.

"Sit," he grumbled. "I'm not going to bite."

I walked across the room and sank into the stool next to him.

"I don't have chocolate or anything, so coffee will have to do," he offered, when I still didn't say anything.

"Huh?" I managed to respond. Articulate as ever.

"For your period," he deadpanned.

God help me, the man was being serious.

"I'm not on my period," I stated sharply.

His face paled in embarrassment. "But last night…" he trailed off.

"I was upset because I found out about the breeding programme," I snapped, "not everything has to do with a girl being on her *period*."

He blew out the breath that he had been holding. Was he nervous?

"This is not going as planned," he muttered.

I poured myself a cup of coffee and stared at him over the rim of my mug, waiting for him to continue.

"Look," he said, "you and I don't have to be friends, but we do need to be civil towards one another."

He looked at me, waiting to see if I would interject or add something. I didn't.

"Partners are expected to complete field assignments together within The Society's humanity projects," he continued.

I raised my brows in surprise. I did not know that we would be expected to *work* together. If anything, I thought he was supposed to serve as some kind of mentor - showing me the ropes, and explaining the intricacies of The Society.

He watched my expression flicker and change, acknowledging my surprise. "Yeah, it was *probably* my responsibility to tell you that."

I glared at him, the heat from my mug warming my hands.

"So, we need to at least be civil to one another and get along for these three months - it's not such a big ask, is it?"

I blew on my coffee before taking a sip.

"What happened to finding other lodgings?" I asked. I knew that I was goading him, but I couldn't help it.

He glared at me in response, and this close, I realised that his eyes, while green, had flecks of gold in them.

"Moving isn't a possibility, so we'll just see out these few months as partners and then we can both move on with our lives."

I smiled, so daddy wouldn't move him. Interesting.

"Okay then," I said.

"Okay?"

"What?" I asked, "I'm not completely unreasonable," I smiled.

He laughed, and the sound wasn't entirely unpleasant.

"I won't be around here much though," he added, as an after-thought.

"Why?" I blurted out, before I could think before I spoke.

I shut my eyes at my outburst, and was only met with laughter.

"I was serious about the bed. My feet hang off the end and I really don't get much sleep, so I'll be making my own way."

I jutted my chin out and declared, "I don't feel sorry for you."

He laughed once more, and all his warmth was making it incredibly difficult to remember that he was an asshole.

"Aria, if I thought for one minute that I could *guilt* you into giving me the main bed, I would have done that already."

A knock at the door broke the warmth and friendship we were enjoying, and without either of us saying a word, the door opened to reveal Joshua.

"Look at the two of you, having coffee in the kitchen together like the civilised individuals that you are," he goaded.

"Hi, Joshua," I said.

"She speaks!" he jokingly clutched his chest in shock.

I rolled my eyes and caught Ajax's grinning face. He shrugged in response.

"Jokes aside, as delicious as you look, Aria," Joshua's eyes travelled up and down my body, taking in the cherry red outfit in all its glory, "duty calls, I'm afraid."

He sighed dramatically, and I realised that if the situation was different, I would want to be friends with someone like Joshua Penn.

Ajax tapped the counter, waving as he followed Joshua out, but before the door closed entirely, Joshua gave me a flirtatious wink, and I simply raised my mug in salute. I wasn't an idiot; I was fairly certain Joshua flirted with *everyone.*

I hardly saw Ajax over the following few days, and after having a somewhat reasonable conversation with him, I couldn't tell if I was disappointed or delighted. That in itself spoke volumes of where my mindset was. I was all-over-the-place-confused; I mean, I wasn't even sure I wanted to work for Saxon and Saxon anymore. Because what did they expect of me? Did they expect *anything* of me?

Because of the system that The Society had set up, I didn't know what my true value was in the world, which just made me ring with disappointment within myself. How had I not noticed this sooner?

Ajax was actually true to his word and hadn't spent a single night in our suite.

"He's all over that dating app," Raquel told me helpfully over breakfast. "I actually think he swipes right and exits the compound to have some fun."

"Are we allowed to leave the compound?" I asked, squinting my eyes at the sun.

Raquel had insisted on sitting outdoors, and like the idiot I am, I had allowed her to position me in the seat that faced the sun directly.

She grinned at me knowingly whilst I simply slid my Tiffany glasses onto the bridge of my nose and huffed out my irritation.

"Are we allowed to leave the compound?" I asked.

"*We're* not allowed to leave the compound, but Ajax? Yeah, he can leave because he's an instructor and he is here pretty much every summer doing training and assignments."

I humphed a non-committal reply.

"Why?" Raquel eyed me. "Do you want to leave the compound so that you can have some fun?" She goaded me, wiggling her eyebrows suggestively.

"No!" I declared quickly.

"And what are you two ladies talking about?" Joshua Penn had somehow happened by our table.

I had 'run into' him a few times over the last few days, and this time seemed to be no different, although judging by how much effort him and Raquel were putting into *not* looking at one another, I knew he wasn't really here for me. He was just a big talker.

"How your best friend likes to swipe right and play outside of the compound," Raquel fired back.

Josh grinned wickedly and leant forward across our table to pick up a grape off of Raquel's plate and pop it in his mouth.

Raquel blushed, and I decided to save her.

"Can you stop being a pervert for more than five minutes at a time, or is that simply not programmed in your DNA?" I barked.

Josh swivelled his head in my direction and smiled. "I think you and Ajax will have fun together."

"What?" I spluttered.

"I meant on your assignment," Josh offered, "you have fire - it'll be good for him to be knocked off of his pedestal."

"You know that you're right up there with him?" I offered.

This time, Joshua's smile grew wider. "Ah, but I don't have nearly as much pressure riding me as Ajax does, which means that *I* am able to get away with a lot more."

He winked at Raquel and sauntered away.

"Bye, ladies," he called over his shoulder.

"Okay, firstly that was *weird*, and secondly - what is up with you and him?" I demanded.

Raquel sighed, her shoulders slumping forward.

"We hooked up last summer," she offered.

"Obviously." I gave her a bland stare in return.

"And I won't allow it to happen again."

"Why? Was it bad?" I queried.

"God, no," Raquel offered, "it's just that Josh has a very specific type of girl he'd want to settle down with, and to be that type of person, I would have to give up on my own dreams and ambitions, and I'm not sure I want to even consider that."

"Does it need to be a serious thing, though?" I asked.

"Society guys tend to get pretty serious, pretty quickly when it comes to those within The Society." She shrugged. "Plus," she added, "I don't even know if we're even compatible in this programme, so it's best we just don't repeat our experience and that way no one gets too involved, or too committed."

I eventually broke the silence by asking, "and what did he mean by Ajax being under pressure?"

Raquel gave me a look that told me I was being an idiot.

"Ajax is Benson SinClaire's *son*," she emphasized, "he will be expected to tow The Society line, settle down, produce perfect little Society babies and still go above and beyond for The Society - he has less of a choice than we do."

I stared at Raquel, suddenly understanding that I wasn't alone in how I was feeling. That it *was* unfair.

"We shouldn't be talking about this," she muttered under her breath.

We finished the remainder of our meal in silence, each of us consumed by our own thoughts.

CHAPTER EIGHT : DATE NIGHT

There is something about a Friday that speaks of freedom, letting loose and *living* - even if you're a grown ass adult with commitments the following day. It is as if a switch in us has been inherently programmed to kick into freedom gear as the last school bell of the day rings.

Our first Friday after a week at The Society compound was no different.

We met in Joe's pub and began the night with a round of cards that soon had us betting and wagering for the most ludicrous items.

Mack had wagered a pair of crocs that his parents had gifted him, arguing that they had never been worn, nor would they ever be worn by him.

At some point, Marissa joined our table, perching herself on Mack's lap. She was witty and dished out snark and sarcasm as good as any of us, and for a moment, I pitied her for being dragged into our world. I pitied her choices being denied to her, and I did not for one moment think she fully understood what she had committed to until it was too late - because once you were part of The Society you could not leave. It was either this or death.

That thought sent shivers down my spine as I pondered whether they would actually *kill* someone for trying to leave. I wouldn't put it past them. Trying to shake off the heaviness that had settled within me due to my thoughts, I walked to the bar for a refill. It would be a champagne evening until the end.

A shiver of awareness ran across me as I stood in line, waiting for service. I looked behind me, trying to figure out if I was just being paranoid, or if there was indeed someone watching me. Based on my first encounter with Ajax, and the rumour mill that went into full swing after that, it wouldn't be entirely impossible.

His eyes met mine from the darkened booth across the room. I could *just* make out the figure that was Paul seated next to him, and Josh was leaning against the padded bench across from him. His gaze held mine for a minute before his gaze dipped lower, taking in my dress.

It wasn't revealing by any means. The emerald green dress boasted a boat neckline, capped sleeves and sat just above my knee, but it was skintight, leaving little to the imagination. My skin was flaming under his gaze, and I had to remind myself to breathe. In the week that I had known him, we had gone from hating each other, to being civil, and not once had either of us looked at the other like this.

It must have been the atmosphere, because Marissa was suddenly grinding on top of Mack as the low thud of the music seemed to thread its way through the crowd. With effort, I turned my gaze away from Ajax and received my refill.

A felt a hand press lightly against my lower back and my body stiffened as an automatic response.

Standing next to me was Paul, his large hand splayed across my back, edging *just* on the right side of going too far south.

I gave him a bland smile.

"Paul," I greeted as I shuffled away from him slightly, causing the distance to be too great for him to maintain that level of contact without it becoming awkward.

"We have a wager," he whispered into my ear, "about who exactly is on your matchmaker's list."

"Oh?" I asked in surprise.

"I think you and I would be wholly *compatible,*" he continued, and the innuendo was not lost on me.

I spluttered a laugh.

"Does that actually work for you?" I asked, aghast.

Paul had the decency to blush as I shook my head and shouldered past him towards my table. As I glanced up at the room, I found Ajax's eyes still on me, and I simply raised my glass in acknowledgement in his direction. He dipped his head in response.

Civil. We could do civil. We had to do civil. Because anything more and anything less was a problem.

I suddenly found myself wishing that he had found entertainment outside of the compound that evening.

Our card game bled into karaoke as we all took turns on the stage. I sang Hotel California to a crowd full of swaying people and realised that Ajax was no longer there - while I was busy having fun; he had left - and in truth, that was probably for the best.

My feet were sore, but my heart felt far lighter than it had all week. Giggling with Raquel down the hallway, I eventually stumbled into the suite. The lights were all off, and I slipped my shoes off and groaned in relief at the sensation of my bare feet against the wooden floor.

I tiptoed softly towards my room, but stopped as I heard the sound of light snoring coming from Ajax's room. Without really meaning to, I was crossing the room and peeking in through his doorway.

There, sprawled awkwardly across the bed, lay Ajax. His feet stuck out at the end of the bed, and his arm hung off the side. I don't think I truly understood how big and built he actually was until this moment.

The white vest he was sleeping in stretched across his chest, highlighting every curve and dip. The man clearly spent a lot of time training.

Not wishing to get caught in the act of watching him, I quickly retreated and put myself to bed. No doubt, in the morning I would have a pounding heachache, but now? Now I felt free, and I did not find it necessary to think. It was as if each anxiety inducing thought was simply spirited away, giving me no time to truly hold and examine those thoughts, punishing myself for the emotions they in turn provoked.

I tumbled into dreams of darkness, and green eyes flecked with gold that had me turning away and seeking them out simultaneously. My confusion had crept into my dreams, muddling all in its path.

Laughter. Male laughter. That was the first noise that filtered to me from behind my wooden door. I lay still for a bit whilst my brain orientated itself with my body. My head throbbed, but not half as badly as I was expecting. I lifted my arms above my head and stretched, testing out the feeling of my body - searching for aches and pains that inevitably came with a night out. Nothing - my body actually felt reasonably *okay*.

I braced myself as I opened my eyes. The headache was there - above my right eye. Sighing, I swung my feet over the edge of the bed and resigned myself to the fact that only water and painkillers could save me now.

I walked into the kitchen with the sole purpose of getting myself a glass of water. My cottonmouth screamed with need as I only half-looked where I was going.

"Well, good morning to you, sweetheart." Josh purred at me from the kitchen counter.

I screamed in fright and may have jumped off the ground a little.

He chuckled in response, the comic that he was.

"Why," I asked before taking my first sip of water, "are you in my kitchen?"

"I'm not here for you, sweetheart - I'm here for him," he said, his eyes tracking someone behind me.

I spun around, far slower than I should have been - fucking champagne - and found Ajax standing in the kitchen, fresh from a shower with a towel slung across his hips. His chest was chiselled and sharp, his six pack abs rippled in the light, and deep vees leading beneath his towel.

Realising where my eyes had gone, I blushed furiously, whilst he only smirked in response.

"Tell me sweet, sweet Aria, do you always wear such enticing clothing to bed?" Joshua asked.

My brow creased in confusion as I looked down at what I was wearing. My white tank top was virtually completely sheer, and in my inebriated state, I put on a pair of black boyshorts.

"Fuck," I muttered, glaring down at my chest, nipples fairly visible through the shirt.

Both men chuckled at my hungover state.

I grabbed my bottle of water and retreated to my room.

"Fucking champagne," I muttered.

"You're going to need some headache tablets," Ajax called after me, laughing.

"I'll get them later," I volleyed back before I shut my door.

Both Joshua and Ajax had seen my nipples. My mother would have been mortified, but I simply wasn't able to find it within myself to be embarrassed. I showered and dressed quickly, only to emerge at lunchtime. Apparently, I had slept the entire morning away.

Mom: Honey, we haven't heard from you. Just checking in to see if you are okay.

This was the sixth message I had received from my mother this week, and I just couldn't bring myself to reply. I felt her betrayal bone-level deep, because despite it all, she was my mother and it had been her job to protect and prepare me. Instead, she sent me to the pack of wolves with little to no information.

I found Raquel sitting at the outdoor restaurant overlooking the pool.

"You missed quite the show," she greeted me.

I sat down, immediately filling my cup up with coffee.

"Ajax and Josh were here doing training laps in the pool, in fact," she pointed towards the health bread that I liked, nudging it in my direction, "there were a bevy of girls lined up just ogling them."

After seeing Ajax's chest, I wasn't surprised.

"Ajax and Josh both saw my nipples," I said.

Her face dropped before she broke out into a grin.

"Not what I was expecting, but I'll go with it - how, pray tell, did this exactly happen?"

I lay my head on the table and groaned at my own damn stupidity.

After giving Raquel a full explanation, she was still here laughing at me, her shoulders shuddering, each time she drew up a mental picture.

"It's not funny," I groaned.

"Oh, on the contrary," she said, wiping the tears of laughter from her eyes, "it is *very* funny."

She took a sip of her orange juice. "In fact," she added, "that story of yours may have made me coming back here worthwhile."

"Why aren't you hungover?" I demanded.

"Because I can hold my liquor," she snarked a reply.

I heard the tread of footsteps before he spoke.

"I much prefer what you were wearing earlier." Josh's voice crooned from next to the table.

I gave him the finger, but in truth, there wasn't much bite in the gesture.

Both Josh and Raquel sniggered, with Ajax Sliding in next to Josh. I swear, the two were joined at the hip.

"A band shirt?" Josh laughed again, pointing at my black shirt and denim shorts.

"What?" I defended. "Metallica is a great band."

"You just don't seem the type," he volleyed back at me, but his eyes never really strayed from Raquel.

I slumped my head back onto the table. "Go away," I moaned at them.

Once more, I was met with laughter. I needed to go back to bed and emerge on a different day, when my head was less sore.

CHAPTER NINE : COMBAT TRAINING

As the following week rolled around, The Society introduced combat training into our schedules.

It had been explained to us all that we needed to be able to, at least effectively, defend ourselves, because at the end of the day we were connected to The Society, and in many ways that made us targets simply by association.

Naturally, some of the attendees had already received various levels of training through their parents in a parental bid to keep them safe.

So, of course, my parents' bid to keep me sheltered. Combat or defensive training was never on the cards for me. Instead, I was shoved into dance recitals and learnt how to pose pristinely for photographs.

Paul had brought in a combat and military instructor called O' Grady. He was tall, built, tattooed, muscled and swore a lot. His light hair was styled messily, and I knew that I wasn't the only female in the room that was eyeing him appreciatively.

The Society controlled the military. While that wasn't a surprise, I learnt that they actually controlled military and government units across the globe - except for China, and I wondered if China was the only country that was truly free. Perhaps we had been willfully misled?

We descended beneath the building, which seemed to house an enormous basement area, kitted out specifically for military training. None of us were really aware that there was even space underground. Although, I should not have been surprised.

The ceilings were much higher here than an ordinary basement, and one section had been entirely enclosed with glass walls separating the shooting range.

I marvelled at the setup they had here. A large gym area had been outfitted, along with a boxing ring set to the side.

Another open area with floor to ceiling length mirrors mounted across the wall stood empty. This was where O'Grady and Paul stood, awaiting our arrival.

Raquel stood next to me in skin tight silver work out wear - a two piece set with three rows of straps on the sports bra that was intricately designed. Looking at the mirror, I found Joshua and Ajax leaning casually, and suddenly understood why Raquel was looking as sexy as sin.

My own gym outfit was tame by comparison. A deep garnet red, two piece. Nothing over the top. The sports bra held my breast firmly, offering a hint of cleavage and nothing more.

"Right," Paul announced, clapping his hands together as everyone gathered closely.

"O'Grady here is going to train you. *All* of you will do this session of basic training where we will grade you in terms of your existing skill level. For those who have a bit more experience with defensive training, we will be moving you out into different sections of the basement."

People began muttering their consensus, while I heard a few grumbling that such an exercise was a waste of time. I had zero training, so I could hardly argue with what Paul was saying.

I found Ajax's eyes in the mirror, watching me. It seemed that he and Josh were simply observing and not participating today. *Great.* One more person who will see that I don't know how to throw a punch. I swallowed down my frustration and anger at my parents and simply looked forward.

"You've done training here before, right?" I asked Raquel.

"Yup." she popped the 'p' on the word.

"Then why are you doing it again?" I asked.

"Because how else will anyone see this outfit?" She grinned at me.

My laughter bubbled out of me in response, causing both O'Grady and Paul to glare in our direction.

The lesson began with us jumping on the spot, and then switching over to jumping jacks, sit-ups and push-ups. Apparently, stamina was important in both defense and combat, which meant that we were all slick with sweat.

I could only thank myself for going to the gym as religiously as I had - albeit, the exercise had stemmed more from the need to *look* a certain way under my mother's influence than actual defense or combat training, but I was still grateful.

Only once we were all panting, O'Grady demonstrated the stance we all needed to be in to go through a punching routine.

I sought out the two figures leaning against the wall in the mirror. Ajax's face was turned toward Joshua's, deep in discussion, while Joshua's gaze was planted firmly on Raquel.

I tried to mimic O'Grady's stance. I had once taken a string of kickboxing classes with my trainer, but this was wholly different.

Before I was even aware of what was happening, O'Grady slid up behind me, placing his hands on my hips to widen my stance, all the while still calling out the combination of "one-one-two."

His hands lingered slightly before gripping my arm, pushing my fist through the process of punching.

"You're too tense," he said, his voice hoarse and low. "You need to loosen up a bit for any of these exercises to be effective."

I nodded my head, unable to formulate a response whilst his hands were still on me, and as I lifted my head up once more, it was Ajax's eyes that were on me through the mirror.

O'Grady grunted his response and moved on to the next person who required assistance.

"The two of you need to stop eye fucking each other through the mirror - it's distracting," Raquel chimed in.

"That is not what we're doing," I hissed, still keeping up with my punches.

"Really?" she asked, "Then pray tell, what *are* the two of you doing?"

I clamped my jaw shut and ground out, "we're being *civil.*"

She glanced sideways at me, knowingly.

"Well, if he's being *civil*," she emphasized, "then I'll take some of his civility."

She winked, and I groaned.

"Says the person who's butt Josh's eyes have been *glued* on," I threw back at her.

She giggled, "he has been looking at me, hasn't he?"

"Less talking ladies," Paul barked in our direction, as we threw ourselves into some more punching combinations.

At some point, Ajax and Joshua had peeled themselves off the wall and entered the boxing ring.

I only noticed because of how hushed the room had become, and when I turned around, I understood why.

Josh and Ajax were shirtless, strapping up in the ring. And for a minute I had thought that my hungover self had imagined his abs and chest, that I had over-inflated them somehow. But the truth was - I had not. Josh, for all his smirking and posturing, was equally built, and I wondered what the hell The Society had the two of them doing to look like *that*.

Refusing to be a spectator, ogling them with a few of the other girls, I turned back to find that O'Grady had dismissed us, with the promise of seeing us again tomorrow. Apparently, this training would become a daily practice.

I grabbed Raquel's arm and tugged her along with me. It wouldn't do for Joshua to catch her staring, and retreated from the basement area. I heard the sound of a boxing glove hit flesh and instinctively turned back, only to find O'Grady now in the ring, flat on his back with Ajax grinning like a maniac. His eyes met mine, and I thought I saw the slightest dip of his chin in farewell.

We retreated back upstairs where Raquel suddenly did not seem half as confident as before.

"Look, let's just get showered up and meet in the cafeteria - we can get a head start in the lunch run."

She shot me a grateful smile as we parted ways.

As I stood beneath the warmth cascading down my back from the shower head, I realised that I had actually enjoyed training. And I wanted to do more of it. I *wanted* to learn how to fight.

The cafeteria restaurant was still fairly empty by the time we re-emerged. Raquel appeared more put together, and I wondered what about the situation downstairs had shaken her.

Mack followed shortly, sporting a blue eye and cut lip.

"What happened to you?" I asked, aghast.

He shrugged. "I was in the ring and didn't block correctly."

Raquel's lips curled up in amusement as he sat down at our table, pouring himself a glass of water.

"You could at least shower *before* joining us." I scrunched my nose up in distaste.

He flipped me the bird and began dishing himself up a plate off of the large antipasti platter in the center of our table.

"Don't let Mack fool you," Raquel chimed in, "the boy can fight."

He shrugged off the compliment. "I've been doing boxing since I was five - my dad insisted upon it."

I realised in that moment that that was what I had been missing from my parents. Sure, they cared for me, but in the same way one cared for an investment. They were always more concerned about their image and 'how it would look' than what was actually good for me. And, I realised that despite being offered everything on a silver platter, I was living an echo of a life, because I hadn't really been loved unconditionally, and the choices I thought I had been making for myself, were hardly choices at all.

"You have a brother, right?" I asked, breaking myself out of the downward spiral of my thoughts.

"Yeah," he grinned, "two years younger than me and not half bad at boxing."

"Oh?" I raised an eyebrow.

Mack nodded. "Yeah, when I started training at five, he began at three - because anything I did, he *had* to do as well, and so my dad ended up training a five-year-old and three-year-old simultaneously"

My lips tugged in a smile as I realised that The Society wasn't *all* bad - some families in The Society were happy and wholesome.

We ate in companionable silence, each of us content to fill our stomachs in favour over talking. Occasionally, Mack dabbed his lip, but for the most part, he actually seemed *okay*.

A messenger dressed in black slacks, a white dress shirt, and black waistcoat made a beeline for our table. It would have been easy to mistake him for a waiter, but the waistcoat gave him away, well, that and the determination of his gait.

We all watched him as he came to a standstill at our table, pulling out a long, crisp white envelope from behind his back.

"Miss O'Luc?" He inquired.

"Yes?" I breathed easily, my manners taking over as my nerves kicked in.

"This is for you." He handed the envelope to me, ensuring that I had a grasp upon it before he fully released the paper.

"Please, be on time," he said by way of departure, and left.

I glanced at Raquel and Mack, and then back down at the envelope.

Mack shrugged, while Raquel said, "It probably has something to do with your assignments."

Shaking off my nerves, I peeled open the envelope and read:

Meeting: 2pm, Small meeting room F4

Attendees: Benson SinClaire

Sarah Lipson

Ajax SinClaire

Aria O'Luc

Discussion: Assignment one

"Wait," I said aloud, "is this today?"

Raquel leant across the table, grabbing the letter from me and scanning through it. Her lips pressed together in a grim line.

"I would wager that the meeting is today," she offered.

I glanced at the time. It was 1.30pm.

"Shit," I said, standing up, "I have to go."

Both Mack and Raquel nodded at my departure as I left to navigate where the hell meeting room F4 was.

CHAPTER TEN : THE ASSIGNMENT

I stood outside the meeting room door, my palms clammy. A draft breezed through the hallway, and I shivered in apprehension. Wrestling for control over my emotions, I gave myself a mental once-over and a pep-talk. I could do this. I *could* do this. There was nothing to freak out over - I didn't even know what the assignment was yet. I wore a bright yellow sundress that sat just above my knee. I had paired it with a denim jacket, and while I would have given anything for more time to have dressed in business appropriate attire, but I would take some hope from the colour I was wearing.

I had arrived five minutes early, but I could not stand outside in the hallway indefinitely. I knocked twice - as was polite - and heard the deep voice of Benson SinClaire rumble, "Come in."

The door swung inwards easily, and I found myself standing in a small room with a circular table positioned at its center. Four chairs surrounded the table, three of them occupied.

Ajax shot me a strained smile, immediately raising my hackles. I smiled blandly in reply. Mental memo received: we were playing this guarded.

"Miss O'Luc," Benson gushed, "please, please take a seat."

I nodded politely and lowered myself next to him. I was seated between Benson and Ajax, with Sarah Lipson sitting directly opposite me.

"I hope my son has been treating you well?" Benson enquired, and out of the corner of my eye, I saw Ajax school his face into a bland expression.

"Wonderfully, thank you," I replied.

"Good, good," Benson nodded, looking down at his notes.

We sat in an uncomfortable silence before Sarah Lipson launched into her speech.

"How much do you know about human trafficking?" She stared at me, her beady eyes tracking mine for any small movement I may emit.

"Um," I glanced at Ajax, but his eyes were firmly planted at a watermark on the table, "that it's a horrific practice that still happens today?"

I spoke the words as if they were a question, but they were not a question.

I was met with silence until Sarah spoke once more. "Yes, it is completely abhorrent that these practices are still in play today."

I breathed a sigh of relief that I did not even realise I had been holding. On some level, I had been worried that they did not stand for human rights - well, not fully anyway.

"We are fighting to dismantle a lot of these systems, but as I'm sure you can imagine, this type of work is conducted discreetly and under the radar - so to speak." Sarah offered me a small smile.

"These kinds of operations form a large portion of our humanity projects that The Society is driving. We have already done so much, but there is *always* more - *always* someone bigger and nastier than the previous guy."

She allowed what she had said to hang in the air before she spoke once more.

"We have a lead on one such trafficking organisation that we believe is holding a number of missing girls and women," Sarah continued.

I shut down the rising nausea that accosted my senses as I thought of those women and children, and what they were most likely subjected to do.

"We were hoping that you and Ajax would handle this matter as your assignment and uncover where these girls are being held, so that we can relocate them to safety," Benson added.

I watched in fascination as Ajax clenched his jaw, his eyes still fixed to the table.

"You don't wish to see them removed to a place of safety?" Benson called out Ajax.

"Of course I do, Sir." Ajax barked, his eyes darting up to meet mine briefly before looking at his father.

"Good," Sarah cooed, "but it won't be an easy task, and I need to make sure that the two of you are up to it."

She looked at me, her beady gaze narrowing upon me, as if I would be the one to somehow say that I was *unwilling* to help those women and children in need.

"I am willing to help," I spoke softly, "but," I hesitated, unsure if what I was about to say would be deemed smart or cast me as completely incompetent, "I am not sure that I am the ideal candidate for this job."

Benson's booming laughter shook the room, and I felt the large sting of his hand as he slapped my back. I braced my hands against the table so as to not rock forward.

"My dear," he gushed, "don't you worry about that, Ajax here has done a number of rescue and retrieval missions - he can show you the ropes."

I glanced at Ajax in surprise. He gave me a tight smile and a small nod.

Watching our small interaction, Benson added, "Ajax is being much too modest. He has been a true hero to many of these women in saving and relocating them. His work at The Society is invaluable - isn't that right, my boy?" He asked Ajax directly.

Ajax shrugged good-naturedly, and something within me settled at seeing that gesture.

"It won't be easy," Sarah added, veering us back on course. "The first meeting is only to discover *where* these women are being held. The two of you would then have to infiltrate the premises to see the layout and setup *before* we plan the rescue mission, and from there, we can send a handful of people in to assist with the retrieval. By my estimate, it will be a three-part exercise."

I sat quietly, my hands in my lap, still unsure what role I would have to play in all of this.

"So, what is the first part of the process?" Ajax crossed his arms, leaning back in his chair, he seemed perfectly at ease - in control even.

Sarah smiled at him, and there was something about the smile that was feral. I chided myself internally for being so jittery.

"We have a man operating on the outskirts of the trafficking ring. You need to meet with him to discover the location of where they are being held, as well as gain any additional information from him about the safest way of entry into their premises," Sarah explained.

"And when we are done getting information from him?" Ajax asked carefully.

"Leave him," Sarah said, "he is one of our own."

It took perhaps thirty seconds for that information to sink in.

"What?" I spluttered, unable to curb myself. "You were going to kill him?"

My shock must have been evident on my face, because Sarah raised herself to her full height, and despite her small stature, she was intimidating.

"If he wasn't one of our own, and was in fact a *human trafficker*, then yes Aria, we would have killed him. Would you rather we leave him to carry on *trafficking?*" She hissed.

"No." I swallowed down the bitterness that had risen in me. "I just thought such an introduction might have been included in your *lectures*," I spat.

I would not be belittled by this woman nor dressed down in a manner that made be feel incompetent. If I was ignorant where it came to *who* The Society murdered, then that was their fault.

We stared at each other, until Benson interrupted, "is this going to be a problem?"

I swallowed once more, my eyes seeking out Ajax's. He looked both amused and sad - I did not even know how that was possible.

"No," I said, "it won't be a problem because he is one of our own - right?" I challenged Sarah.

"Right," she nodded, seating herself once more.

An uncomfortable silence settled upon us once more.

Ajax cleared his throat. "So, when are we meant to meet with him?"

"Tomorrow around noon," Benson offered.

Ajax and I both simply nodded our consent.

As Ajax and I both headed towards the door, Benson called towards me, "Oh, and Aria?"

"Yes?" I swivelled in his direction.

"I think this goes without saying, but this assignment is *confidential*."

I nodded. Got it. Don't talk about the assignment.

I did not see Ajax for the rest of the day, and when I saw Raquel and Mack later in the day, and they queried what the meeting was about, I smiled blandly and told them that it was just about our living arrangements - about how Ajax and I needed to make it work.

Mack laughed in relief, but I had a feeling that Raquel was still skeptical.

As I settled into our suite for the night, there was still no sign of Ajax. I was left with my own swirling thoughts for company.

The Society was not inherently good. I knew that they wouldn't be. I knew that you didn't obtain that level of power and wealth by towing the line - but murder? I exhaled, reminding myself to breathe. I needed to sort out my conflicting opinions before our meeting tomorrow. While I wasn't a soldier, I had read enough strategy books to know that a conflicted person in battle was more likely to get themselves killed.

And this was a battle of sorts. I needed to get through these next few months to regain my freedom - the pieces that I had.

The Society murdered people, but did they only murder human traffickers? I didn't know. Was I okay with them murdering human traffickers?

I allowed that thought to sit and stew, steeped in the questions of 'whose child is he? Who's brother is he? Who would miss him if he were gone?'

I drew a bath and allowed my muscles to relax and simply soak as I sorted through the fragmented thoughts of my mind.

But wasn't the act of dismantling human trafficking oragnisations noble? Weren't they actively saving people? And it was Ajax Saving people - not some nameless person I didn't know.

While Ajax certainly wasn't my favourite person at the best or times, I also did not believe that he was bad or inherently evil. Although he was far deeper involved with The Society than I initially realised.

The Society was actively helping people - and did that not count for *more* than the fact that they eliminated those who were committing these crimes.

The problem, I realised, lay in the fact that The Society was too powerful, and them choosing to snuff out lives just simply placed them in the category of a body with too much power - too much influence. Because what really gave them the right to take a life? Who made them the judge and executioner? Or was it simply a self-proclaimed role?

I watched in fascination as the bubbles swirled in the bathtub, ebbing and flowing with my movements.

While my thoughts were still muddled, the warm water served the sole purpose of relaxing me. Perhaps I did not need to have my thoughts exactly figured out? Perhaps I could hold them in reserve and wait and see what exactly The Society was about. There would most certainly be aspects about The Society I wouldn't like - the question was: would I be able to live with them?

And if I decided I couldn't live with what The Society was doing? What then?

It wasn't as if you could just decide to *leave*. It did not work that way.

Knowing that not much else would come from these recurring thoughts, I decided to turn in for the night, briefly wondering where Ajax was and whose bed he was warming.

None of my business. I mentally berated myself and shut down those thoughts in their tracks.

I tumbled into dreams filled with Ajax and I driving a jeep across a cornfield, gunning it to save someone.

"She's not worth saving!" Ajax yelled at me. But in that panic fuelled dream, I wouldn't listen.

"Everyone's worth saving!" I yelled back, the wind whipping through the crops, the entire field bending and swaying in an eerie way.

Suddenly, his hand was pressed against my inner thigh, and I wanted him to kiss me. As his face drew closer to mine, I watched in fascination as our breath mingled, forming a dark grey cloud.

His nose nuzzled my neck, and everything within me wanted him to touch me - consume me.

A loud blaring sound drew me away, and before I understood what was happening, I had slipped from Ajax's arms and was switching my blaring alarm off.

Frustrated, I huffed into my pillows. I liked dream Ajax, but judging by how much of an asshole he was in everyday life, it was probably better that I stamped those dreams out in their tracks.

It had been too long since I had been with anyone, and I supposed being surrounded by testosterone fuelled men that were shirtless half the time was not helping my libido.

CHAPTER ELEVEN : THE MEETING

I descended into the basement for an early session of training with O'Grady. In lieu of our confidentiality agreement when it came to the assignment, both Ajax and I had to continue with our day as if everything were entirely normal.

Which placed me firmly in front of O'Grady, who appeared to have some bruising on his cheekbone.

He stood in front of me, molding my body into the correct position for another round of punching combinations.

"Should I ask what the other guy looks like?"

I knew that Ajax had knocked him down, but I hoped that he had a few more rounds with some of the others that resulted in that bruising. I needed to somehow cast Ajax in a good light, because without that, I wasn't sure I could go ahead with the assignment - no matter who we were saving.

He shrugged good-naturedly, "He knew my weaknesses, and I was an idiot and forgot."

Within this close proximity, I watched his Adam's apple bob as we swallowed, swivelling my hips into the correct stance. I smiled at him and was suddenly aware of a presence creeping up behind me.

"I need to take Miss O'Luc to the shooting range, so the positioning won't be necessary." Ajax spoke from behind me and I saw ire flash in O'Grady's eyes before he released me.

I pivoted and came face to face with Ajax. He smelt of soap and after-shave.

"We're shooting this morning?" I stared at him in disbelief. Asshole.

Ajax merely nodded.

"Like an actual gun?" I asked again, needing to clarify.

I heard O'Grady's bark of laughter to my left as Ajax laughed. "Yes Aria, like an actual gun," he mimicked.

Giddy with excitement, I skipped after him, causing a few of the other guys to chuckle.

"You're going to need to at least be able to shoot a firearm for this assignment," He whispered under his voice.

I blanched, "As in for today?"

"No," he snapped, annoyed, "not for *today*, but as quickly as possible."

We took the last remaining steps in silence before I replied, "all righty then."

Before we walked through the wide glass doors, Ajax placed a pair of bright orange ear muffs on me, double checking that my ears were indeed covered. I didn't think his partner having her eardrum blown out would be a winning situation, and so, despite the seemingly kind gesture, I knew that at the end of the day; he was looking out for himself.

Asshole.

Once the glass door swung shut behind us, all sound from the outside world seemed to evaporate.

Ajax positioned himself behind me, and I shivered involuntarily as the warmth of his body pressed against mine. His arms dipped across my chest as he positioned the gun in my hands, ensuring that I was holding it correctly, and that I could essentially aim the thing.

"See that target there?" He whispered in my ear.

I simply nodded, my head hitting his chest in reply.

"We're going to start easy, just aim for *anywhere* on the white sheet," he said.

I nodded once more and lifted the gun in line with the center of my body. I used both hands to steady the shot, as instructed, and when I pulled the trigger, I felt the air whoosh out of me as the bullet flew towards the target.

And missed entirely.

I tried again. And again. And again.

I wish I could say that due to the divine genes that The Society had orchestrated, I was somehow gifted with the ability to be an incredible marksman straight off the bat, but that wasn't the case. Not in the least.

Not once did I even hit the sheet of paper, causing Ajax to frown, scratch the back of his head and say, "Okay then, we'll try again tomorrow."

"How important is it that I am able to handle a firearm for this assignment?" I asked in defeat.

He flashed me a smile. "You'll get it right, and until then, I will have your back."

I shouldered my self-disappointment and followed Ajax out the basement. We needed to get ready for our meeting.

We both had been briefed on what was expected of us, and how to look and act the part. Although, I very much doubted that Ajax needed to be briefed.

We were seated side by side in the backseat of an SUV, and I swallowed down my nerves as I struggled to truly wrap my head around what we were driving into.

"Why aren't we driving ourselves?" I asked hesitantly.

"Because it's always a good idea to have a seperate get-away driver in case shit goes wrong." Ajax answered without lifting his eyes off of his phone.

I sighed heavily, sinking back into the seats of the SUV. My leg brushed against his and I pulled my thigh away suddenly, not really wanting to be seated within such close proximity.

"Relax," Ajax said once more, his eyes glued to the screen of his phone. "I won't bite, and you are not even remotely my type."

"Wow," I grumbled, "you really know how to charm a girl."

I didn't want to be his type. But, I also did not want to *not* be his type. I was confused.

"Aria," he spoke sharply, placing his phone in his lap, "we are partners on an assignment, nothing more and nothing less. Now, I'm sorry if you have glided through life on those model looks of yours, but you are not my type - you are too naive and stuck up to be anything remotely more than frigid. You are like a little fawn thrust into this world, and somehow you are seemingly shocked by everything. I'm not here to hold your hand and guide you through life. I am simply your partner in this fucking buddy system. That is all." He seethed, his eyes piercing mine.

My cheeks flooded with embarrassment. Is that how he saw me? The equivalent of some rich child with no true life experience? It stung deeply. And maybe that was because it was largely true.

"Just so we're on the same page," I spat, "civility does not equate to me *liking* you. I am so grateful that I am not your type, because the last thing I would want to attract in this life is an asshole like you."

He glared at me, the waves of anger rolling off of him and hitting me in the gut.

"Then we are in agreement," he seethed.

"It would seem that way," I muttered.

The drive was completed in heavy silence, although I doubt Ajax even noticed as he was on his phone the entire time. In response to the awkwardness, I pulled out my own phone, deciding to reply to my mother.

Aria: You should have told me.

I fired the text off. Following it with a second.

Aria: I walked in here completely blind.

Before I could spiral too deep into the rabbit hole of anger towards my parents, the SUV rolled up a gravel pathway to a large ranch.

"Where are we?" I leaned towards the window, looking around.

"We're in the small town of Buda." The driver answered.

Before I could even reply, Ajax was out of the car, walking towards the ranch house by himself.

He was a prize asshole. And worse yet, he didn't give a shit. I scrambled out of the car, power walking to catch up with him.

"We're just here to get information," he muttered under his breath, as if I were a complete moron in need of coddling. Fuck him, actually.

He rapped on the door three times before a gorgeous caramel coloured man swung open the door.

"Trigger," Ajax greeted him.

"Jax," he smiled, "you're early, and," he glanced towards me, "you've brought company."

"Oh?" Trigger queried. "It seems they have upgraded the partner system since I was last there."

"Nah," he shrugged, "she can't even shoot a gun."

I blushed furiously. A fucking asshole. That's what he was.

"Well, that's not a requirement for what I have in mind." Trigger grinned wickedly.

"I am standing *right* here," I ground out.

Ajax simply laughed, dismissing my anger, and stepped through the doorway.

Asshole. Asshole. Assshole. I kept repeating the word over and over in my mind.

Trigger led us to a room that had been fitted with a large desk, with two guest chairs placed next to one another.

"So, what information do you have for us?" Ajax jumped right to the point.

Trigger's back was turned to us as he took his time pouring us each a glass of whiskey.

"Always in such a rush," he goaded in reply, "No, *Hi Trigger*, or *How are you Trigger*."

Ajax grunted non-coherently as Trigger handed him his glass.

Leaning against the desk, Trigger looked us both over.

"You're going to need her to get some of the information," he finally spoke, his hand moving marginally to indicate that I was the 'her' he spoke of.

"Once again, I'm *right* here," I spat.

"Walk me through the setup," Ajax continued, ignoring me entirely.

"The setup is big," Trigger confirmed, "the only way that you're going to get in is as a client."

I sat in silence, trying to fully grasp the situation, promising myself that there would be time to tap into my anger.

"They run an elite brothel - specifically for the girls that they don't sell. So, you would have to enter as a client. I can get you a booking and that way you can gain access."

"But?" Ajax drew the word out, pushing Trigger to continue with what he wasn't mentioning.

"But, even as a client, you would only be privy to the front-end of the operations, not the back-end - not where the girls are being held, their living conditions and how many they still have."

"What aren't you saying?" Ajax asked carefully.

"I'm saying," Trigger's eyes darted towards me, "that she can cover the back-end and you can enter as a client. That way, you would be able to get all the information you want, as well as scope their premises. Fucking brilliant actually, if you ask me"

"What does that mean, exactly? Go in the back-end?" I interjected.

Trigger looked at me and turned back towards Ajax to answer.

My hand wrapped around the glass and without giving it a second thought, I threw the glass towards Trigger. He jumped out of the way without a millisecond to lose.

"Fucking hell," he exploded.

I stepped towards him and watched his shoulders tense in response.

"While I appreciate that you don't know me," I spoke softly, "I am on this operation as well, and *I* will be the one entering the back-end. So, I would appreciate it if you didn't dismiss me as some silly little plaything that you can't be bothered to answer."

Trigger stood stockstill, as if waiting to see what else I would do. He nodded once and took a step towards me. It was my turn for my shoulders to tense.

"You don't want to be treated as some irrelevant play thing?" He spat. "Well, that's exactly the role you will need to play if you have any hope of gaining information from the back-end."

"What do you mean?" I asked, the panic rising within.

"I mean," he smirked, enjoying my discomfort, "that the only way to get you in will be as one of *his* girls. And even then, the chances are slim."

"Fuck," Ajax barked out.

"Yeah," Trigger nodded in his direction, "and it doesn't help that your girl is a hellcat."

I shut down the panic and asked, "What does being one of his girls entail?"

He laughed humorlessly, while Ajax remained silent.

"It means that you will be treated as a brothel girl while you are there."

Before I could formulate a response, Ajax angled his body between Trigger and I.

"When can you get us in?" He asked.

"Probably a week from now," Trigger replied, "but your girl is going to have to go in first, so that when you arrive, she is already in."

"Thanks for this, Trigger," Ajax nodded. "The Society owes you one."

"I'll collect that debt when I need it," he replied, handing Ajax a thick folder - no doubt filled with the information we needed.

"Oh, and Aria?" Trigger grinned at me.

So, he did know my name. Why was I always surrounded by assholes?

I turned to look at him, my face blank of any expression.

"If you ever feel like *playing,* I would gladly tangle with you. I like my women with a bit of fire in them."

I flipped him off and walked away to the sound of him chuckling.

Assholes. Assholes everywhere.

As the gravel crunched beneath our feet, I turned towards Ajax and said, "I don't like him."

"Duly noted."

CHAPTER TWELVE : THE REPORT

Once again, I found myself waiting outside the door of F4. The only difference this time, Ajax stood next to me. Later, I would examine all of my mixed emotions and re-examine the words he threw at me in the car, but now I needed to remain calm. We were expected to debrief Sarah Lipson and Benson SinClaire on the information we had received, and from there, plan the second leg of this assignment.

I didn't quite know what to make of the information Trigger had handed over, and I did not really know how I felt about what would be expected of me. *Numb.* That was what I felt, and I briefly wondered if the girls that they held captive felt the same way, or if they even had the luxury of allowing themselves to feel. Were they drugged? Were they lucid? How many men did they get passed around to? And what about the younger girls? Were they in waiting or used just the same?

These thoughts sickened me, but they were necessary. Realising and understanding what was happening was necessary, because if I couldn't even acknowledge what was happening around me, what hope did we have of saving them?

The door opened to reveal Benson, his top shirt button undone, giving one the illusion of casualness. Nothing about that man was casual, and his grim expression terrified me.

"Please sit," was all he said as Ajax and I found the same seats we had sat in the day before.

"So," Benson said, "what did you find?"

Ajax spread the file out across the round table and studied its contents before talking.

"The head of the organisation is a man who goes by the name of Soldero Rodrigues," he offered, "but from what this states, he rarely visits the brothel, choosing to only involve himself in the actual sale of the girls."

Benson grunted his disapproval whilst Sarah pulled a face of disgust.

"His operation is run from the warehouse district just outside of downtown Austin, and you can only gain access through booking an appointment."

"And that's to be *serviced* by one of his girls?" Benson clarified.

Ajax grunted his agreement.

"Is that how you're getting in? With an appointment?" Sarah asked.

Ajax nodded, "Yes, Trigger has arranged it for next week."

Benson and Sarah shared a look that sent shivers scuttling down my spine.

"But with the appointment, you will only see what they *want* their clients to see," Sarah stated. "Presumably, the information we need won't be available to you - the girls in captive will be hidden somewhere."

Ajax shot me a pointed look, and I knew that if I wanted to have any say in the matter, now was my time to speak.

"I will be going in as one of Soldero's girls - a new acquisition perhaps," I stated.

Sarah scrutinised me, looking for any holes in what I had said.

"That's actually bloody brilliant." Benson said gleefully. "As one of his girls, you will see the intricacies of his operation from behind the scenes."

I nodded whilst Ajax sat stone faced, sipping on a glass of water.

"And if they decide to test out their new *acquisition*?" Sarah asked.

This was the question. This was what I had been grappling with. Going in under the pretense of being one of the girls who serviced men at the brothel was one thing, but in doing so, there was the risk that I would actually have to *service* someone. But to not place myself in that position meant that I was willfully leaving those other girls there to endure all manner of abuse.

"Well then, I suppose I will be getting laid," I said crassly.

Ajax coughed, spluttering his water at my response, whilst Benson clapped in delight.

Sarah's expression was taut as she added, "then you will need to visit our health facility. We have developed an injection that will prevent you from all sexually transmitted diseases, and as we don't know Soldero's view on protecting his 'acquisitions', it will be better to cover ourselves."

I nodded my understanding, before allowing my thoughts to flow forth, "If you have developed such an injection - why doesn't the public have access to it? It would resolve so many health complications."

"Because it hasn't been green-lighted yet for the public," she answered matter-of-factly.

"But why?" I pressed.

Her displeasure was evident at being questioned, but I refused to back down. This is what I couldn't understand about The Society - on the one hand, we were saving women from human trafficking rings, and on the other we were denying the public access to revolutionary medicine.

"Because it needs to go through the bidding process first," Ajax interjected, the gold flecks in his eyes more evident with his anger.

"Back to the matter at hand," Benson steered our conversation back towards Soldero, "how much earlier will you be going in than Ajax?"

I glanced towards Ajax, hoping that he could provide the answer.

"An hour," he stated.

Benson nodded, "all right, so there's a good possibility that you won't be required to partake in Soldero's business, but there are no guarantees."

I dipped my chin in agreement.

"More important than gaining access - how are we going to get you out once you have the information that you need? Soldero isn't going to let one of his girls simply walk out," Sarah cautioned.

"I'm going to buy her," Ajax stated.

We all looked at him. He was stark raving mad.

And an asshole. I couldn't forget that.

"And if they don't let you buy her? If they don't put her up for sale?" Sarah countered.

"We will just have to make him a very satisfactory offer that will allow me to buy her. We will ensure that refusing it would make no financial sense whatsoever."

Sarah glanced at me and then back at Ajax.

"Look at her, Ajax," she demanded. His eyes suddenly remained fixed to the table.

"Look at her," Sarah demanded once more.

Ajax's eyes rose to mine, and a flash of emotion flickered across his face - too fast for me to determine exactly what it was. Regret perhaps?

"He is going to look at her and realise what a prize he has on his table. She will fetch far more on the blackmarket than your offer, so there is a very real possibility that he will turn down your offer. What then?"

"Then we *retrieve her*," Ajax seethed.

"And, once again, I'm right here," I said, dissipating the building tension in the room.

"Do you have any idea what he will see when he looks at you?" Sarah swung her eyes towards me. "You have a model physique, you are attractive in all the ways that men like, and make no doubt that if they see what is beneath your clothing, getting you out will be a near impossible task."

"Do you not want us to complete the assignment?" I asked her.

"On the contrary, I think this is the best opportunity that we have to get those girls back, but we also need to be realistic about what we're walking into so that we can plan properly," she shot Ajax a disapproving look.

"Fine," I blew out, "So how do you get me out if they don't accept Ajax's offer?"

"We have a retrieval team on standby," she said - as if it were the most obvious thing in the world, and to her, I suppose it was.

Benson let out an impressed whistle, and I shot her a grateful smile.

"Soldero does not get involved in the day-to-day operations of the establishment, so there is a very good chance that his manager -" he glanced down at the file quickly, searching for the name, "Samuele Diaz, will gladly accept the financial exchange for her," Ajax added.

"Is that a risk you are willing to take?" Sarah asked, "Are you willing to risk her simply to prove that you're right?"

I suddenly did not despise Sarah so much as I watched the muscle in Ajax's jaw tick.

"No," he ground out.

"Wow," I said, "that must have been difficult for you to admit."

Ajax shot me a look, whilst Benson glanced at us questioningly.

"Are we done here?" I asked, causing all three of them to look at me.

"Y..yes," Benson nodded.

"Thank you," I said as I brought myself to my full height and left them to their discussion. I had no doubt that more planning would ensue, but I was done simply allowing this life to press upon me with no say in how I wanted to live and what I wanted to experience.

I hated that Ajax had been right about me - I was so fucking naive, but there had also been a willingness to that naivity - as if I knew that if I looked up my entire world would shatter, and so I willingly kept me head buried in the sand, blind to things I simply did not want to acknowledge.

I needed to start taking greater control over my life - even if that control could only occur within the boundaries of The Society.

It was already pretty late by the time Ajax and I returned to the compound, but I was not in the mood to be surrounded by anyone else. I needed to sit with my thoughts and my shortfallings by myself.

Without giving much thought about where I was heading, I descended into the basement. A few people lingered, but I wasn't here for them. I thought I saw Paul and Josh in the ring, but I couldn't stop to look. I could not stop, because I needed to vest some sort of control over my life.

O'Grady was stationed at the shooting range, and after giving me a quick rundown on safety guidelines, he placed me in a booth armed with earmuffs and a standard issue firearm.

Inhale, exhale, straighten arms, widen stance, aim, shoot on exhale.

Again.

Inhale, exhale, straighten arms, check stance, aim, shoot on exhale.

Again.

Again.

Again.

With each bullet that I released, I felt lighter.

I was not some pampered, privileged princess with no will of her own. I was more than an aggrevation - a silly little burden to be dealt with, and fuck Ajax for making me feel that way.

As I worked through my anger on the shooting range, my aim slowly became less poor. I was actually hitting the sheet of paper - granted; I wasn't hitting any vital body parts displayed on the sheet, but I was at least making holes on the damn thing.

At some point, O'Grady crept into my booth, laying out another round of ammunition. I reloaded and continued, content to lose myself in the exercise.

Just because I had been sheltered and was somewhat naive in my views and understanding of the world, did not mean that I deserved to be silenced, demeaned or disregarded. I had grown up watching my mother all too eagerly take her place in society, where she only spoke things that were practiced, lest she looked like an idiot.

I was not my mother. And if that was what The Society was looking for, they would have to find someone else. My unwillingness to simply *accept* everything had always been there - and I willfully ignored it. Not anymore. Never again would I bury my head in the sand.

As I released the last bullet, I felt somewhat lighter. I did not know how long I had been there for because I had lost myself at the handle of the gun - or perhaps I had simply found myself.

Once I laid down the gun and exited from the shooting range, I found Ajax leaning against the wall, waiting for me.

He straightened once he saw me, and I simply shook my head. I couldn't deal with him now. I *wouldn't* deal with him now, because quite frankly he was an asshole who didn't deserve my time. We would work together, because it was expected, but I was not going above and beyond the call of duty for Ajax SinClaire.

CHAPTER THIRTEEN : MAPPING IT OUT

The following morning, I found a large folder detailing a list of missing persons, their last locations and last recorded clothing that they were wearing - all of them were female.

My stomach churned as I understood what I was looking at. A folded, cream-colored piece of paper sat next to the file.

Aria

Have a look through this file and glean as much information from it as you can.
You may encounter some of these girls on the next leg of our assignment.

Ajax

PS: you're right, I am an asshole.

I scrunched the letter in my hand and sank down onto the floor, pulling the file onto my lap as I looked through it meticulously.

That is how Ajax found me, sitting cross-legged on the floor with sheets of papers spread around me. A pen and pad in my hand as I jotted down notes.

None of this made sense. As I looked down upon the photographs of these missing girls and women, I knew that if something had to happen to me, my parents would pay whatever they had to to get me back. Hell, my father would probably buy out every billboard in our state simply to advertise that I was missing, along with a hefty reward.

These women didn't have that privilege, but they had me, and I was going to do my absolute best to free them. It felt somewhat fitting that my first true act, that I was doing of my own accord whilst opening my eyes to the world around me, was actually freeing people.

It is a funny concept to be owned. Can you really own someone? Their thoughts? Beliefs? Opinions? Emotions?

Some may call that indoctrination, but what the law brought it down to was the forced limited movement of an individual. *Physically* restricting someone's movement and who they interacted with. Of course, once this was achieved, I supposed that you could then force that person to do your bidding - and that varied according to ownership.

Dark curly hair and bright brown eyes stared back at me from the page.

Alessandra Mikinos

Aged 19

Last seen wearing jeans and a blue shirt walking on her way home from bible studies.

Date missing: 12th May

A small blonde girl smiled up at the camera, her blue eyes blinding in their brightness. She was beautiful in her fragility.

Gillian Jones

Aged 17

Last seen wearing jean cutoffs and a white top leaving her boyfriend's house.

Boyfriend is the main suspect.

Date missing: 30th April

Another photo jolted out at me, possibly because she looked so much younger than the other girls. Straight, dark hair cascaded down her shoulders, her eyes lit mischievously as she stuck her tongue out at the camera.

Andrea Larson

Aged 15

Last seen wearing black leggings and a long band shirt while walking home from school.

Date missing: 15th May

My hands shook as I created columns along my blank page. There had to be some sort of commonality amongst these girls - some connecting factor that might give insight as to why they were taken.

I divided the information up, categorizing the regions they were taken from, the dates they were taken and their ages.

The women ranged in age from fifteen to twenty-three. They were all either middle class or came from impoverished backgrounds, making the ability for their parents to fight back and spend on extensive searches impossible. They came from all different regions and states, meaning that the operation was far greater than I had even realised.

Newspaper clippings accompanied their photographs and missing poster sheets. One article speculated that the young fifteen-year-old - Andrea Larson - had run off with a band, influenced by rock music and the devil. Another clipping was an interview with her parents, her mom begging anyone with information to come forward, while one of her teachers pegged her as a 'teen with troubles'.

It sickened me that a young teenager was missing, and the media had somehow still spun it in a way that she was the problem.

Gillian Jones' boyfriend had been brought in for questioning and released due to a lack of evidence. The entire newspaper narrative pivoted on the fact that she went to visit her boyfriend at his house, with her own mother being quoted as saying, "I told her that nice girls don't visit boys at their homes, but she did not listen. And now? Now we pray to God for her return."

In each piece that I had read, the media famed the girls as somehow at fault for their own kidnappings - some even questioning outright if they had even been kidnapped.

Even Alessandra - who had been walking home from her religious studies group - had been cited as having recently started a new relationship with a boy, thus being the reason for her downfall.

A dark-skinned girl with huge eyes smiled shyly at the camera.

Lisa Barnard

Aged 18

Last seen wearing a denim dress heading towards the subway.

Date missing: 23rd May

According to the news reports, no one was surprised that Lisa had disappeared, with a 'friend' of hers saying, "it's clear that she doesn't want to be found and that doesn't surprise me, she always thought that she was better than everyone else."

"What are you doing?" Ajax asked, hovering at the entrance of our suite.

"Did you know," I said by way of greeting, "that all of these girls went missing just before summer?"

"Um…" Ajax offered, scratching the back of his head in confusion.

"Because," I pressed on, "by the time summer rolls around, these girls are long forgotten. I mean, who would want to be concerned about some missing girls when summer activities are booming?"

"How about the police?" Ajax offered blandly, clearly not impressed with my line of thinking.

"Yes, well, obviously the police - because it's their job, but not the public."

"What do you mean?" He asked.

"I mean," I huffed out in irritation, "that the timing can't be a coincidence. They *all* went missing a month or two before summer."

He just looked at me, and I growled in frustration. How could he not see this?

"That means that the media will give these women a few weeks worth of attention before they are fully focussed on *summer*, and even those who may have taken a public interest in the story - well, their attention will be lost because their kids will be home from school, or they will be planning a vacation. And suddenly, this missing person's story is no longer relevant - not to the public at least."

"May-be," Ajax offered, dragging out the word, as if he were truly considering what I had just said to him.

"They seem pretty well organised - everything I can see has them picking girls up from all over the country, and the only connecting factor I can find between the girls is this loose timeline."

"It would also make sense to grab them just before summer - because if they need to travel to sell them, it would be easier to accomplish in peak season when it's crowded," he added, thinking out loud.

"Have you gone through all of them?" He questioned, surprise coloring his tone.

"No," I shook my head, "I'm still busy."

Ajax took two steps forward and slung his jacket over the closet chair, before lowering himself onto the floor next to me.

Some of my dark strands of hair fell into my face as I glanced at him in surprise.

We stared at each other for a beat too long before he said, "Hand me a pile that you haven't looked through yet - we can work together."

"Y… you'd help me?" I stuttered.

His grin could bring a woman to her knees, and I acknowledged then just how dangerous Ajax could actually be.

"We're partners, right?"

I frowned at him, refusing to simply forget how much of an asshole he had been.

I couldn't throw it away simply because he was being nice to me, or because he acknowledged what a giant dickhead he was in his note. Call it self-preservation if you will, but I held the memory of asshole Ajax close, because this nice Ajax? He was far more deadly to me.

"Come on, Aria," he goaded, "let's just start over and be civil towards one another."

"Civil?" I choked on my laughter. The idea seemed so absurd. "Didn't we try that already?"

He grimaced slightly. "Yeah, okay, fine. I'm an asshole - but you're no prize peach yourself, Princess, so let's just start over as friends."

"Friends?" I asked, looking up at him.

"Friends," he nodded, "It can't be such an impossible task."

I absorbed what he said for a minute. I didn't want to be friends with him. Actually, if I could have nothing to do with Ajax SinClaire, I would be ecstatic, but those were not the cards we were dealt.

"Fine," I muttered, "but I still think you're an asshole."

"Duly noted," he said.

We sat in silence, working through the file spread before us. As time for dinner rolled around, Ajax simply arranged two pizzas to be brought up from one of the restaurants so that we could continue working.

Two hundred and thirty-one.

That was how many women were crammed into the file - how many had been plucked from their lives for the sole purpose of human trafficking. And they had all been taken between April and May.

As I stared down at our list, my heart clenched.

"They can't all be at Soldero's brothel in downtown Austin," I said, trying to fit all the pieces together, puzzling out the truth.

"No," Ajax said, his voice gruff with realization.

"Where else could they be?" I asked him, searching his flecks of gold for the truth.

"I don't know," he whispered, and I wondered if he wanted to free them just as badly as I did.

"Do you think we'll find them all?" I asked, needing some sort of reassurance.

He closed his eyes. "We are going to try," was all that he could offer.

The silence felt heavy, but not uncomfortable, as we contemplated what we had both committed to.

"I didn't expect you to agree to the plan... I mean the brothel and everything that goes with it," he said quietly, leaning his head back against the couch.

"Of course I would agree," I grumbled, indicating towards the pile of papers now neatly stacked on the floor.

"Why wouldn't you think I'd agree?" I looked at him, and with the light cast across his face, he looked so much more vulnerable than the asshole Ajax I had become accustomed to.

"Asshole, remember?" He smiled teasingly.

"Can't argue there," I smiled back.

CHAPTER FOURTEEN : MENTAL FLEX

Over the next few days, I tried to stay focused on our daily routines and the general task at hand, otherwise I would drive myself insane with thoughts of posing as a brothel prostitute and possibly sleeping with a stranger. I settled on the fact that it was no different to having a one-night stand with a stranger, but even I didn't believe that lie.

My aim with a gun was becoming better, and while I was still not a great shot, I was a hell of a lot better than when I began - I chalked it up to spending hours at the shooting range daily.

As the day of the second leg of the assignment crept closer, I came to peace with the fact that I might have to actually have sex with someone completely unknown to me - worse yet, under brothel conditions. This fact was only further cemented when I had to visit the compound's medical center for the preventative vaccination that Sarah had arranged.

The cool white leather of the medical bed seemed to stick to the underside of my thighs as I shifted uncomfortably, waiting for the on-site doctor to administer the injection. My nerves jangled through me as I wondered if this injection was even safe - I mean, all I had was the say-so of Sarah Lipson.

Too late now, I suppose.

Before my thoughts could take a downward turn, spiking my anxiety, the doctor breezed in.

Her chestnut coloured hair was twisted into a neat chignon, her white scrubs offsetting her dark complexion nicely.

"My name is Doctor Leila Oswaldo," she greeted me with a bright smile, and that small act of kindness put me at ease.

"Aria," I said by way of introduction.

"Okay, so this is going to sting a little, but honestly, it's one of the best things we've created so far. Life changing, actually," she gushed.

I nodded through my deep breaths, in and out. I had never been a fan of needles.

"Clever," she smiled, looking at the small all-seeing eye tattoo I had on my wrist. I shrugged back, refusing to break my deep breaths for speech.

I felt the small sting, and then it was over - just like that.

"Okay, we're done. Do you want to know all the diseases you are now protected from?" She sounded almost giddy.

"Um… sure," I said. I could hardly refuse the knowledge, even if it should have been something I asked *before* receiving the shot.

Leila went on to list a string of sexually transmitted diseases, and I found myself slightly grateful that I did not know the full extent of the list beforehand, because if I had, I would never have had sex.

"How long am I protected for?" I asked hesitantly.

"Forever," she grinned broadly at me, and I found myself wanting to be friends with someone like her. That longing only made me miss Nats more, and I wondered if she would be okay by the end of summer.

I did not see Ajax as I left the compound, a sleek black sedan once more waiting for me. The drive was over far too quickly, with the driver depositing me right outside Trigger's ranch.

He stood on the front porch waiting for me and I quietly had to remind myself that he was part of The Society and that I was safe. But that statement was laughable, because what did safety really mean in this context?

He ushered me indoors without a word and once I was safely tucked away from the rest of the world, he looked over my appearance and deftly handed me a cotton sack filled with clothes.

I peeked inside the bag.

"No," I stated, handing the bag back to him.

He chuckled darkly, "Well, you're not going to get in with what you're wearing," he spoke honestly.

I sighed loudly, "I get that - but does it have to be *that?*" I asked, gesturing towards the bag he now held.

"Oh, I'm sorry," he said sarcastically, "women brought into forced prostitution through human trafficking don't usually have a say when it comes to their attire."

I narrowed my gaze at him and grabbed the bag.

"Bathroom's down the hall," he grinned triumphantly.

The denim skirt rode up far too close to my thighs for my liking, and the leopard print cut off shirt sat *just* below my breasts. In fact, if I stretched my arms in the air, you would definitely see some under-boob.

The gold belly chain was the last item, with charms dangling from it depicting the moon, sun, and stars.

He gave me a light grunt after looking me over, and something within me loosened at that fact, because despite being an asshole, he wasn't going to try anything. His gaze softened as understanding skittered across his face.

"You're right not to trust them," he spoke softly, in fact, if I had not been standing right next to him, I would have missed it.

I glanced back up at him, about to question what I had heard, before he quickly pressed a finger to his lips in silence. He leant forward once more, dipping low so that he could whisper once more.

"Everything we do is monitored, so think before you speak because you are never really alone."

I nodded in understanding as Trigger hearded me towards his van.

"It's showtime," he stated loudly, "are you ready?"

"As ready as I'll ever be."

"Then turn around," Trigger grinned manically.

I held my wrists together behind my back as Trigger twisted the rope around my arms, joining my hands together.

I maneuvered myself into the back of the van and tried to sit down delicately - a near impossible feat with my short denim skirt. Trigger paid no notice to my dilemma and simply shut the back of the van, shrouding me in darkness.

Because there were no windows at the back of the van, I could not even brace myself for the bumps - simply because I could not see them. When Trigger opened the back door of the van, he found me sprawled across the floor.

A Latin looking man stood next to Trigger, grinning in delight.

"You didn't lie about this one," he spoke with a lilt to his voice.

Trigger grunted in response, pulling me out the van by my tied wrists.

I blinked back at the light flooding my senses, tears pin pricking at the corner of my eyes. We were standing in a deserted gravel lot that stood behind a large warehouse. A neon sign hung to the left of one of the large orange roller doors, flashing in time with my heartbeat.

*De*fault it blinked in and out, beckoning all to come and see exactly what a warehouse filled with women had to offer.

Trigger handed me over without a word, shooting me a weighted look that sought to question if I was, in fact, okay.

I tried to convey that I was fine, and on some level it must have worked, because he turned away from me, shutting the doors to the van as I was tugged across the lot and into the warehouse.

"Samuele is going to be fucking smiling when he sees you," he grunted, pushing open an interleading door that revealed an enormous well lit room. At the center of the room stood a large raised square platform that was knee height. Pillows and cushions, in varying shades of blue, red and orange, were scattered across the raised podium. With a series of chandeliers hanging above the podium, shattering the light into a million different directions. If it had not been crafted on such a large scale, it may have almost been romantic.

In the darkness of the room, booths had been created, shielded by Moroccan room dividers. The sweet smell of vanilla wafted faintly into the room, relaxing in a way that certain smells often were.

Before I could truly absorb what I was seeing, I was being dragged through a side door and down a darkly lit passage.

This. This was where all the things they didn't want their customers to see happened. We walked past one door that was cracked half open, and I heard a woman sobbing hysterically.

He noticed where my gaze had landed and smiled. "Sometimes," he spoke into my ear, sending shivers of repulsion through me, "we have to give the girls a… cocktail, to help them relax a bit more, and sometimes, some girls take longer to adjust than others."

I felt the deliberate brush of his lips against my ear, and it took all my willpower to not turn around and push him away.

"You're not going to need a cocktail, are you?" He continued talking softly into my ear. "No, you're going to be a good girl. Not *too* good though, I don't mind a *little* fight."

We passed two more closed doors before another man emerged out of the next one. He was tall with broad shoulders, a receding hairline, and a potbelly.

"Raul," the man barked, and suddenly he was no longer whispering into my ear anymore.

"Look what I have, boss," Raul spoke from behind me, shoving me towards him.

I stumbled slightly from the momentum, and the man brought out a hand to steady me. Dark black eyes raked over my body as he took me in.

"Well, look at you," he smiled.

Fear curled into the pit of my stomach as I realised that I was standing before Samuele.

His eyes snapped back at Raul as he spoke. "Get her ready for our first round of appointments for today."

My stomach sank.

"Boss?" Raul asked hesitantly.

"We'll put her out on display in the open room, and test her - she'll bring us good money," he spoke as if I were a prized race horse.

"Who will be testing her, sir?" Raul asked as his hand trailed below my skirt.

I reminded myself to breathe as I aimed to steady my nerves. Panic would not serve me now.

"Did you oversee the deal with Kulig?" Samuele gave Raul a dark look.

"Yes, Boss," Raul answered from behind me.

"Good," he said, "then you can test her."

My heart sighed in relief and then revulsion. I was relieved that I did not have to sleep with Samuele - I had found everything about him oily and abhorrent. But was I happy that I would be having sex with Raul? Whilst it was hardly a hardship to look at him, he was still part of a human trafficking ring, making him the lesser of two evils.

Samuele slipped back into the room, shutting the doors quickly behind him. The miniscule glimpse I did get showed rows of shelving, with boxes stacked neatly on top of one another. They looked like the same ammunition boxes we had back at the compound, but I couldn't be sure.

We had passed four doors thus far, and I made an effort to keep a mental map of this place.

The door to the last room was flung open at the end of the hallway. It was brightly lit. A woman in dark cargo pants and cascading dark curls stood at the center barking orders amidst the chaos.

There appeared to be twelve women - in some sort of state of undress, surrounding her.

The woman's eyes darted towards Raul, and she smiled warmly.

"You bringing me gifts?" She asked throatily.

"We have to have you ready for the first round of appointments - we're going to be showing her off," Raul offered.

"You bring me a canvas like this and showing her off is not a hard feat to accomplish," she said. Her gaze sought out any flaw that I may have.

She reminded me of an agent I once met, when I was fifteen, who offered me a modelling contract. Of course, my mother vetoed the whole thing once she heard that there was a good chance that my nipples would be on display during fashion week. Because heaven forbid.

I wonder what she would say now about her daughter entering a brothel.

CHAPTER FIFTEEN :
SHOWTIME

"My name is Manuella," the woman greeted me as Raul retreated, "and it's my job to make sure that you're ready and willing by the time our attendees arrive.

I pushed down my worry and panic and stared up at her.

"You ever done this before?" She eyed me carefully.

I shook my head, unable to formulate words.

She began making fast work in untying my wrists, and when I could suddenly feel my hands once more, she spoke the command, "Strip".

The handle of her gun stuck out from the waistband of her pants, and as I looked around the room, I realised that I had been mistaken initially, and that there was another dressed woman in the room.

She wore a long black ACDC band shirt, moving from woman to woman, applying body oil and makeup to each one.

"Undress now," Manuella snapped at me, frustrated that I was clearly taking too long.

I shoved my panic down as I shimmied out of my skirt, revealing a thin, white g-string. I lifted the leopard print shirt over my head, revealing my breasts.

Manuella gazed over me methodically before stepping forward and releasing my hair from the ponytail it was in.

"Andrea," Manuella snapped, and before I realised exactly what was happening, Andrea Larson stepped before me. She looked thinner than what her photographs had portrayed and she was sporting a splotchy blue bruise on her cheek.

She gave me a grim smile before kneeling before me, lathering body oil up my legs.

"Andrea?" I asked, forgetting myself for a minute.

Manuella's head snapped towards mine, sending me a disapproving glare. Andrea shook her head at me and added more oil to her palm.

She worked her way up my body and hesitated by my breasts. I simply held out my palm for some oil so that I could do it myself.

She complied in silence, dripping some oil into the palm of my hand so that I could oil my breasts and nipples up.

Once I was done, Manuella barked an order at Andrea to touch up my face.

And suddenly I understood why Andrea was dressed. She had found a way to be useful outside of servicing the men, and my heart broke a little for the fifteen year old girl who had to be quick thinking and savvy enough to present herself this way.

A low moan sounded from the other side of the room and I glanced over as Andrea painted my lips a bright red colour. I stretched my neck further to try and get a better look and suddenly, I realised exactly what I was looking at.

Alessandra lay on the floor, handcuffed to a pipe jutting out from the wall. Her hair was matted with blood, and her streaked face and split lip spoke of a fight.

These girls were here.

I had to hold that thought close because otherwise, I would break. They were *here*, and we were going to save them.

"Customers are almost here," Manuella called across the room, "you know what you do."

I watched in horror as many of the girls worked their fingers deep into themselves. Soft panting and moaning ensued.

My face flushed with embarrassment as I stood there, unable to look away.

"You're not going to get anywhere with that scrap of material still on," Manuella barked at me, referring to my white underwear that was still firmly in place.

I slid them off, feeling entirely exposed.

"Now, when you get out there, there's no foreplay for you - *unless* the client wants it, but in most cases, they simply want to sink into you, so you need to wet yourself up."

She glared at me when I still didn't move.

"Are you deaf, girl?" she yelled, "or shall I ask Andrea here to help you out with that as well?"

I shook my head and moved my hand in between my thighs.

I knew how to work my body and brought myself to the brink of climax pretty quickly, biting down on my lip so that I wouldn't moan.

I would not give that satisfaction.

I slid the warm slickness through my folds, ensuring that I was well and truly ready for Raul.

Manuella already started sending some of the girls out, leaving me as the last one to exit.

The cool air of the hallway swept against my flush skin, causing my nipples to pebble, and when I emerged into the large open plan room with the raised podium, I understood exactly what was happening.

"Are you willing?" I heard the familiar voice ask, sending relief to flood my body.

"Yes," she purred in return.

"And are you drugged?" Ajax asked as a followup question.

Before I could hear the response, Raul was there, dragging me towards the podium, pushing me onto my hands and knees, the colourful cushions supporting me.

I heard Raul groan in appreciation as he hoisted my ass slightly higher into the air, but I was too absorbed in what was in front of me.

Ajax had a blonde woman spread out before him on the dais, and I could not take my eyes off of him as he slid into her.

As if he was aware of being watched, his head snapped up, his eyes met mine. I heard her moan as she arched up into him, but his brow furrowed as he looked at me, and realised exactly what I was doing.

I gave him a grim smile, with a half-shrug of my shoulder, and then I felt Raul behind me at my entrance and I inhaled my nerves.

He was of average size, but I still felt every inch of him creep into me. And when he was sheathed fully in me, he groaned something unintelligible.

I leant back into him, feeling the full force of him as he glided in and out of me. Ajax's eyes never left mine, and I saw the minute he gave himself over to the moment, thrusting back and forth with meticulous precision. Sweat began to glisten along his chest, and I tracked a bead of sweat as it slid down his abs and into his fierce thrusting.

He watched me watching him as the blonde beneath him spread her legs wider, giving him greater access. He gripped one of her thighs and held onto it as the sounds of her moaning echoed through the chamber.

Raul grabbed a fistful of my hair, pulling my head back, causing me to cry out in pleasure. Ajax's eyes flared with lust and I felt my nipples harden at the pure sensation.

Raul's grunts and the sound of flesh slapping against flesh mingled with the blonde woman's moans. I felt my orgasm build in my core, and could only pant through the euphoria.

The cushions beneath me shifted slightly as a gentleman lay next to us, a fiery redhead climbing atop him.

I couldn't look away as she slid down onto his large cock, taking him all in. She moaned seductively, her fingers pinching and caressing her nipples, and I shut my eyes at what was building inside of me, trying to delay the inevitable.

I glanced back at Ajax, his thrusts wilder this time, but his eyes were still fixed upon me as Raul fucked me from behind. The sensation of being in a public room like this was *too* much.

My breasts swayed with each thrust Raul drove into me, but with Ajax's eyes upon me, I could not delay the inevitable any longer. My climax rocked through me as I moaned something unintelligible. My inner walls clamped down on Raul's cock. I heard him shout out to the Lord before he braced himself against me for support.

I watched through panted breaths as Ajax came tumbling down soon after me, the blonde woman wrapping both of her legs around his waist, meeting him thrust for explosive thrust.

I felt Raul pull out from me, the warmth of him leaking out of me, down my thighs.

"Jenny," Raul called across the room, "clean up here," he demanded, and I watched in blissful fascination as a woman walked across the room, a washcloth in hand.

Raul grabbed the washcloth from her. "I'll do it," he said gruffly.

He knelt behind me and began cleaning and wiping all the evidence of our experience away.

I leant forward onto my elbows, allowing Raul easier access.

"Good girl," he whispered, his hands splayed across my ass.

And still, Ajax did not look away from me - not once. In turn, I watched in fascination as he removed himself from the blonde beneath him.

He was *big*.

Possibly double the size of Raul - maybe more.

When my eyes flicked back up at his face, he had a smirk firmly in place, knowing full well that I had been looking my fill.

I glanced away quickly, blushing. And wasn't that the irony? I had just been fucked by a complete stranger in front of him and *now* I was blushing?

Once I was all clean, Raul lifted me off the dias.

"How much?" His strong voice rang out across the room.

We turned in unison towards a fully dressed Ajax.

"Pardon?" Raul spluttered.

"How much for her?" Ajax stated, his eyes sweeping across my upright, naked form. I didn't miss the flicker of heat in his eyes.

"You can make a booking and request her," Raul said, almost dismissively, turning to leave.

"Not for a booking. How much for her to leave with me today?"

Raul turned back, the sound of those nearing climax filling the air.

His response took too long to be considered polite.

"I will have to ask Samuele to attend such a discussion," Raul finally said.

Ajax nodded, his eyes hovering over me once more.

"Jenny will show you to a meeting room," Raul snapped, "we will be with you shortly."

Everything happened in such a haphazard rush. Manuella squeezed me into a skin-tight short gold dress that boasted a low v neckline, making me fearful of moving *too* much in case one of my breasts bounced free.

Samuele was notified and seemed delighted with the news - which boded well for me. I had to trust in Ajax in this matter. There weren't many other choices. With a last spray of perfume, Manuella sent me out with Raul.

Samuele joined us in the corridor as we walked back through the chamber with the raised podium. A new round of girls were now in the throes of passion, men mounting them as if it were their right.

Another interleading door stood on the opposite side from where we had just come from, and suddenly I found myself in a meeting room fitted with a Persian carpet, a large rounded wooden table with a hookah placed in the center, and a pacing Ajax.

"So," Samuele drawled, "you want to buy my girl."

I saw Ajax's eyes darken at the *my girl* part.

"Yes," was all he replied.

"But you haven't even *been* with her," Samuele countered.

"I've seen enough to know that I want to *purchase* her," Ajax emphasized.

Samuele hummed, shoving his hands deep into his pockets, rocking back on his feet.

"How was your experience with her Raul?" Samuele asked.

"Akin to a religious experience, Boss," Raul replied.

"A religious experience," Samuele repeated.

I simply stood silently to the side, waiting to see how this would play out.

"There are a lot of men who would be willing to pay *a lot* of money for such a 'religious experience'," Samuele said, as if it were merely a thought he was pondering.

"How much?" Ajax said carefully.

Samuele chewed his inner cheek for a bit before replying, "Normally I would ask for five hundred thousand. But for her?" He paused dramatically for effect, "for her I'd take nothing less than seven hundred and fifty thousand dollars."

To his credit, Ajax did not even flinch, simply responding, "Fine."

Even Samuele looked taken aback by how quickly he agreed.

"But," Ajax cautioned, "she leaves with me now."

Samuele, already doing mental calculations, seemed to be getting excited by the prospect of earning that much off of one person.

"Of course, of course," he offered, "but you will need to do the financial transfer before you take her."

Ajax was already pulling out his phone, demanding the account details on where to wire the money.

Raul simply looked across at me sadly, resigned to the fact that (for as far as he knew) I was being sold to a stranger.

I tempered my rising anger as I watched Ajax transfer an obscene amount of money across, simply so I did not have to stay here.

A lump of gratitude formed in my throat, and soon Ajax held my arm, guiding me towards the exit.

CHAPTER SIXTEEN : BACK TO BUSINESS

Ajax drove us back to the compound in silence. There wasn't much for either of us to say at that moment. He had seen me naked, bare and consumed by another, and I, well, I had seen him ravage a woman in the most intimate way possible, all the while staring at me.

I didn't know what to make of that. I didn't know what to think. And I certainly did not know how I felt about *enjoying* my experience. We were supposed to be there in a bid to save those women from the very situation I had just revelled in.

"Let's go shower and change first, before we report back," he spoke softly, as if he needed to be gentle with me. I simply nodded and climbed out of the car.

I stared at my shampoo bottle for a long time whilst the water beat against my skin. It was almost as if after everything we had done, I now felt a distinct disconnect from my body - as if it were no longer my own.

I looked down at my legs, the same legs that had arched and spread in a brothel. I should have felt disgusted - delighted - shocked, but all I felt was numb. And I didn't have to have a psychology degree to know that that in itself was a problem.

Dressed in jeans and a white Ramones shirt, I met Ajax in the living area, allowing us to head towards our debriefing session together. He looked over my outfit, not able to hide the surprise on his face.

"I didn't feel like dressing up," I mumbled, turning my head away to leave.

His fingers slid along my jaw as he gently turned my face back towards his.

"You did so well today," he spoke softly, his thumb stroking my jawline in a back-and-forth motion.

"Did I?" I asked him doubtfully.

"Yeah," he nodded, "because of what we did today, we'll get to save those women, and that's got to be worth something - right?"

I dipped my chin in quick agreement.

Meeting room F4 was quickly becoming a regular fixture in my schedule, which didn't exactly thrill me.

Benson and Sarah were seated - as expected - as Ajax and I stepped over the threshold in unison. Ajax immediately poured us each a glass of water, sliding my glass to me across the table.

None of this went unnoticed by Benson, and I had to suppress my eye roll - it didn't matter where in life you hailed from, your parents would always take an interest in your dating life - even if there was nothing to take an interest in.

"Report," Benson spoke, and it was as if that one word unlocked it all.

Ajax launched into his findings first, detailing additional security cameras that had been outfitted on the exterior walls of the warehouse, which had not been accounted for in the file that Trigger had handed over. He explained the detailed booking and appointment system that they had, and he discussed the existence of boxed shadow rooms that were down a separate hallway, catering to those who wanted privacy. Although, each shadow room had a large one-way mirror that allowed for someone to look in and watch the activities taking place.

He had also placed a few button cameras where he could, in order to track footage of what was taking place at the warehouse. I tried to not let the shock of that knowledge show on my face. It wasn't that I disapproved of the methodology, it was simply that I had not even been aware that that was part of the plan.

As Ajax finished his detailed report, Benson was still taking notes down. The sound of the pen scratching against the paper pad was the only thing filling the room.

"And your report?" Sarah addressed me.

Right. I didn't know where to start, and so I decided to simply walk them through my experience.

"There is a hallway that splits off from my main chamber of the brothel," I said, impressed that my voice did not waver with nerves. Everyone sat quietly to listen to me.

"From what I could count, there are six rooms in total that that hallway leads to. Now, obviously I couldn't see into each room, but there is one area where they place the girls that are having bad reactions to the drugs pumped into their system," I said.

"You saw that?" Ajax interjected.

I nodded, "I heard and saw a girl sobbing uncontrollably and Raul said that she was having an adverse reaction to the cocktail they had given her."

Ajax's jaw clenched as I mentioned Raul's name, but I simply pushed forward, suddenly needing to tell them *everything* I had seen.

"Another room looked like it held shelf loads of ammunition, but I couldn't see what else they had there - so that's a big unknown at this point," I said.

Both Benson and Ajax looked at me in surprise, and some small part of me hoped that they were impressed.

"How did you even see that?" Benson asked.

"Samuele walked out of the room as we were walking down the hallway," I shrugged. "I glimpsed what I could."

Benson nodded thoughtfully, flexing his hand in the air, urging me to continue.

"At the end of the hall is the room that they keep the girls that are in rotation to go out and meet their clients," I spoke with more strength this time.

"How many girls were there?" Benson asked.

"In the room?" I needed clarification.

"Yes," he said, his voice sounding hoarse.

"By my count, there were twelve, but -" I hesitated.

"But?" Ajax prodded.

"But," I swallowed, "Alessandra was there, handcuffed to the wall. She was in the room, but not in rotation."

"Wait," Ajax demanded, "you saw her? What condition was she in?"

I nodded. "She didn't look great. She was bruised, and it looked like there was matted blood in her hair."

Ajax blew out harshly and we all sat in silence for a moment before Benson asked, "did you recognize anyone else?"

"Yeah," I croaked, "Andrea was in the room as well."

I could feel Ajax's eyes on me, as if he could singe the answers from me with a sheer look.

"But," I continued, "I don't think she's *servicing* the men who visit the warehouse, I think she is assisting with the girls' appearance, and that way saving herself from that experience," I explained, although if she had had to endure those men previously, I did not know.

I went on to explain how she was applying makeup and oil to the girls before the clients arrived.

I chewed my bottom lip as I contemplated how to exactly express my thoughts.

"Spit it out," Ajax sighed.

I hated that he knew I was withholding my thoughts.

"I think..." I started hesitantly, "I think," I said, more firmly this time, "that she is deliberately aggravating them so that they lash out at her, making her unsuitable for client appearances."

"Fuck," Ajax said, "are they beating her?"

"I don't know, but she had a huge bruise on her face, and I got the impression that she had allowed it to happen - preferred it even, to being shopped out like the other girls."

"And you got this impression from the whole twenty minutes that you were in a room with her?" Sarah asked, choosing this moment to speak.

I narrowed my gaze upon her. "Yes," was the only response I offered.

"Also," I said, diverting the conversation back towards the actual topic at hand, "the woman who controls the girls is called Manuella - and she is armed."

"Shit!" Ajax exploded. "You met her?"

"Yes - why?" I asked.

"Because she is Soldero's wife," Benson offered, "which means Soldero couldn't have been too far behind."

Ajax absorbed the information with unflinching determination.

"You have no idea how lucky the two of you got," Benson cautioned.

But I did not feel lucky.

I left the meeting as the chord of disconnect wrapped itself around me firmer, causing me to feel both too aware *and* unaware simultaneously.

I went through the motions of the day, smiling when it was required of me, attending lectures and discussions when I was required to, and saying all the right things - because despite my mother's short fallings as a parent, she had trained me well.

Two thoughts swirled at the forefront of my mind: I had enjoyed acting the brothel prostitute (and everything within me told me that this was wrong) *and* I had walked away from Andrea and Alessandra - I had seen them, recognised them, knew what they were subjected to - and still, I had walked away. It didn't matter that I knew we would be going back to save them, because a lot could happen to a person between now and then.

Rationally, I knew that it was more than okay that I had enjoyed myself in the brothel - rather enjoy myself and be a willing participant than the alternative, but rationality had nothing to do with the bevy of emotions that were rising up within me.

I needed to come to terms with my experience and how they measured up to who I wanted to be, in comparison to who I thought I was, and what the world was expecting of me.

If I were in Andrea or Alessandra's shoes, would I forgive me? My stomach sank when I knew the answer would be a resounding *no*. We had left them at the hands of human traffickers to be raped, sold and tortured for a 'bit longer', until we could extract them safely. But what if they no longer cared about *safe* and simply just wanted a *chance*?

I grabbed a bottle of wine from one of the kitchens and went to my room, scooping up a punnet of strawberries and a box of Oreos on the way. I wouldn't be attending the usual dinner rollout. I just needed to not think for a minute, because if I allowed these thoughts anymore legroom, they would drown me. But the thought of allowing myself to be distracted by a crowd of people felt overwhelming. I was too sensitive - too aware to be around people.

Perhaps a night in would do me good. Or, it might tip me further over the edge, but I knew for certain that I couldn't remain downstairs where Raquel and Mack would undoubtedly seek me out.

CHAPTER SEVENTEEN : A NIGHT IN

I shimmied out of jeans, content to hang out on my bed in just my Ramones t-shirt and panties. Pants were overrated anyway. My bra followed suit, landing on top of my crumpled jeans on the floor.

I flipped my laptop open, deciding that getting lost in series with wine and junk food did not seem like such a terrible way to spend my night - especially after the day that I had had.

On some level, I knew that I was unravelling, but I could not find it within myself to care - I had nothing to stabilise myself with, and felt as if the earth was truly lava.

I opened the bottle of wine, swigging straight from the bottle. Because - just as pants - I had decided that glasses were overrated.

I watched reruns of an old time favourite series, allowing my mind to follow the script by heart.

I heard the front door of the suite open and close, but could not be bothered to move. Ajax had probably stopped in to change before he headed out for the evening.

My stomach grumbled, demanding Oreos, despite the guilt I was so adamantly trying to not acknowledge.

"What is this?" Ajax was leaning against the doorway.

I glanced up at him, my right hand still deep within the box of Oreos, and gave him a sheepish smile in response.

"Healthy coping mechanisms?" I offered in reply.

Ajax's frown didn't magic away with my statement as I had hoped. Instead, he stalked towards the bed, as if he were approaching something feral - something in need of taming. But I was so far beyond being tamed that I wasn't sure what he hoped to accomplish.

Even without meaning to, my eyes flicked over him, taking in his black tight, v-neck t-shirt. Unconsciously, I licked my bottom lip, watching the muscles move and shift beneath the black material.

Unbidden, the image of him completely naked, sweat glistening on his chest as he pounded into the blonde beneath him, arose in my mind.

His eyes darkened, as if he knew exactly where my traitorous thoughts had turned to. He swallowed, and I watched his throat bob, as still, he crept closer.

"What are you watching?" He asked, his voice low and gravelly as he sat on the edge of my bed.

I was suddenly all too aware that I was in a set of black lace panties and a t-shirt. My nipples hardened beneath my shirt, the cool white material brushing against them, taunting them under Ajax's gaze.

"How I Met Your Mother," I answered, my voice coming out breathy.

"Shift over," he said softly, and I could not find it within me to disagree. I moved across the bed, making a large space for Ajax as he stretched out next to me to watch the show.

He glanced around in distress at my meager stash of food.

"This is all you have to eat?" He demanded, appalled.

"What!" I defended. "It's not like I was expecting company."

He smirked, pulled out his phone, and began barking a list of food orders down the line.

I was still staring at him when he hung up

"You are certifiably insane." I raised an eyebrow, smirking at him.

"While your series choice is on point, your food choices are questionable."

I folded my arms across my chest in defense.

"We can hardly survive on half a box of Oreos and a handful of strawberries," he countered my silent reply.

"I have wine," I felt the need to add.

He raised an eyebrow, and I hated that it caused a swirling of desire deep within me.

"You have *half a bottle* of wine," he scoffed.

"Fine," I conceded, leaning back against the pillows, suddenly exhausted with this discussion.

He kept shooting me concerned glances, which I chose to ignore, far more interested in the series in front of me.

Twenty minutes later, a knock sounded at the door. Ajax, to his credit, did not even look my way. My appearance and non-verbal responses must have been enough of an indication for him to know that there wasn't a chance in hell that I was going to get the door.

He returned with two large pizza boxes, and a bag full of junk food treats - and an additional bottle of wine.

"Come on," he urged, "it's not going to bite you," he said as he saw me eyeing the pizza suspiciously.

"Why are you being so nice to me?" I uttered, trying to make sense of where asshole Ajax was.

He looked at me for a long minute before he said, "Maybe I'm being nice because I can't get the image of your gorgeous body being fucked in all the ways *I* want to consume you - erasing every place that fuckhead touched you, or maybe I'm being nice because you survived your first assignment and got more information than any of us bargained for, or maybe it's a bit of both."

I sucked in a breath, unsure of how to respond.

"Eat," Ajax said, turning back towards the show.

I placed a piece of pizza in my mouth on autopilot as I rehashed what he had just said.

I placed the pizza back down and turned to him, "but I am not your type," I said in confusion.

His face softened slightly as he looked at me, "Aria, look at you - how can you not be my type?"

His words hung in the air.

"But you said -"

"I said that you're not my type because you are part of The Society, not that I'm not attracted to you," he interrupted, clarifying things.

I looked at him, weighing his words carefully, and realised that he was present in the here and now, and quite possibly, the only person who understood what I was feeling. I didn't need commitment, I just wanted to feel better. I wanted something to anchor me before I gave myself over to the guilt and turmoil that were plaguing me.

I leant forward, my lips brushing his in the whisper of a promise, "You're not my type either."

And suddenly we were a clash of teeth and tongues. We were not gentle, but we were real.

Ajax pushed me down against the bed, demanding in his arrogance. I lifted my body up towards his, biting his lip and drawing him closer.

His groan set fire to my veins as I kissed him deeply. His tongue met mine in a dance for dominance.

Suddenly his hand was sliding under my shirt, pausing as he realised I wasn't wearing a bra.

He palmed my breast, pinching my nipple until an involuntary gasp escaped me. He chuckled against my breath, causing me to shake in anticipation.

Ajax wasn't a mere boy that I had known growing up, and he certainly wasn't the average size of Raul. No, Ajax was all domineering male, teasing me to the brink of oblivion with just his hands and kisses.

"You have no idea how long I've wanted to do this," he said against my mouth, flicking my nipple once more.

"Since you and Josh saw my nipples through my shirt?" I panted the question, struggling to remain coherent.

"Since I first saw you," he replied, his hand moving onto my other breast.

I arched into his touch, panting with need.

"I've got you," he whispered in my ear.

And then he was lifting my shirt over my head, and I couldn't get the damn thing off quick enough.

His lips trailed down my neck, tracking a path to my breasts once more, where he lathered them with his attention using his tongue.

I was in a blissful haze of need and desire, with Ajax being in control of when my pleasure would be met out.

Finally, releasing me from my torturous desire, his mouth slid down to my core.

Sliding my black panties down, he pushed my legs open wider, gripping my thighs evenly.

My hips lifted off of the bed as he wrapped his lips around my clit and sucked. Pure, undiluted pleasure roared through my body, but just before it hit, my body clenched upon itself, my legs aching to close in a bid to deny myself this pleasure. Ajax growled in response, pushing my legs firmly back in place, ensuring that my pleasure was met out justly.

I collapsed back onto the bed, sated in a way that I had not been earlier. The pressure that was Ajax eased off of me as he stripped down with militant precision.

My eyes travelled down his body and rested upon his long, erect cock. This close, I realised exactly how big he actually was, and swallowed in apprehension.

"We doing this?" He asked, his voice low and gruff. I knew in that moment that if I had said *no*, he would have walked out of my room, no questions asked. But I was not ready to give up the feeling of being grounded - the feeling of being centered and somewhat calm, to the point that my own thoughts were no longer raging against the cage of my mind.

And so, I bent my knees slightly, parting further for him in reply.

He grinned, and something about the self-satisfied smile sent a lick of heat through my core.

He leant on the bed, positioning himself at my entrance. Even with just that simple act, I knew - felt - that he was so much more than any of the others, and I braced myself as he slid into me slowly, inch by glorious inch.

I threw my head back at the sheer feel of him invading me. There was a slight twinge of pain, accompanied by the pleasure that was already building in anticipation as I stretched to accommodate his size.

I moaned as he slid back out and then in again, his cock deeply seated within me.

"I wanted to devour you when I heard you make those sounds today," he growled out, "and now - those sounds? Those sounds are just for me."

I could not even begin to formulate a reply as he thrust in and out of me in a punching rhythm. I shut my eyes at the explosive feeling building inside of me.

"Ajax," I breathed, "I'm nearly… Oh God… I'm nearly-"

"I got you," he grunted, lifting my thighs slightly higher, deepening the angle.

I felt myself clench around him as I was nearing my climax.

"Ajax…" I moaned, palming my own breast in sheer desperation at the feel of him.

"Don't stop. Don't stop," I begged, "please, Jax, I'm almost there."

I opened my eyes to find Ajax grinning at me as he fucked me hard.

"You feel fucking exquisite," he growled, and on his next thrust I exploded. I felt my inner walls tighten around him in response and heard him scream "fuck" - but that was all secondary to the stars that were shooting behind my eyelids as I embraced that orgasmic bliss.

Before I had even fully come back to my senses, Ajax was flipping our positions so that he lay beneath me and I now sat on top.

This new angle allowed me to feel every inch of him, and without a word, I began sliding up and down him. I knew why he chose this position - so that after everything we had done today, I could be in control of *this* situation. I could determine how we ended.

His jaw was clenched tight, and I felt the muscles in his legs tense. He was close. I decided to push him over the edge and moved against him faster, rubbing my already sensitive clit against him until I was once again on the brink. I rode him for all I was worth, until he barked something unintelligible as he came in explosive spurts between my walls, and I leant forward into his chest as my pleasure closely followed.

We lay there, him deep within me, tangled up in one another. Ajax lifted his arm above his head and brushed a pizza box.

I giggled at the absurdity of it all, and he flashed me a grin in return, lifting a slice of pizza towards my mouth.

Amusement danced across his face as he watched me grab the pizza slice and eat it, still naked astride him.

Some sauce dripped onto my breast, and before I could even attempt to clean it, Ajax scooped it up with his finger, sucking it clean.

Warmth engulfed me as we were unable to break eye contact, and suddenly I wanted him again.

"Shower," he said in response to my wandering thoughts.

"Shower," I agreed.

As I climbed off of him, and he slid out of me, I felt empty, as if him being inside of me was my very tether to this world.

Before my thoughts could overwhelm me and pull me under once more, he was there, his hand on the small of my back, guiding me to the shower.

CHAPTER EIGHTEEN : NO COMPLICATIONS

His hand never strayed from my back, and once we were both under the warmth of the shower, he caged me in with his arms against the tiled wall, and said, "You know what I realised about you today when we were on the assignment?"

"Hmmm?" I hummed as his hand trailed across my stomach, dipping closer to my thighs.

"That you like it a little bit rough," he whispered.

The combination of his whispered words with the featherlight trailing of his hand had me aching for him once more.

"And do you know what else?" He whispered the question, stepping closer so that his lips were almost against my neck.

"What?" I swallowed as he dragged his fingers through my folds.

"When you climax, you are the most beautiful thing that I have ever seen."

I swallowed audibly and said, "then make me climax." My voice sounded low and sultry - a sound I have never heard myself make before.

Without any more words, Ajax lifted me up, pressing my back against the wall.

"Wrap your legs around me," he grunted.

I listened, obedient only because I knew that I wanted what he was offering.

He pinned me in place, ramming into me with such force that my inner walls tightened around him in the first thrust. He grinned knowingly.

I wanted to be irritated that he was right - that he had read me so easily, but I also very much wanted to be fucked by Ajax SinClaire.

I leant my head against the tiled wall and welcomed his fast thrusts.

"Harder," I panted out as my orgasm fast approached.

And if I thought he could not quicken his thrusts, I would have been mistaken. His hand wrapped around my wrist as he held it against the wall above my head, driving into me time and again.

"Jax," I moaned, my voice echoing off the walls in the shower.

He kept up his pace, and when I could no longer take it anymore, I once again shut my eyes.

"Look at me," he commanded.

My eyes snapped open to his, his golden flecks shone brightly beneath the water.

"I want to see all of you when you come," he growled, not once losing his pace.

He growled as I bit my lip, but I did not close my eyes to him.

We watched each other intently, and with each thrust, I felt my core tighten, building up to the inevitable.

His thrusts became more frantic as he fucked me harder against the wall. I looked down, realising that at some point I had arched into him, my breasts thrust forward and pert.

"Fucking magnificent," he growled as he saw me look down upon myself. He released the hand he had pinned to the wall, and as if knowing that I needed something to push me over the edge into oblivion, he slapped my breast, watching it bounce back up in place.

My spine tingled as my core tightened, and suddenly I was moving against him, his eyes watching my every movement.

"Jax, Oh Jax, Oh Jax," I chanted his name so that the words ran into one another. My nails dug into his shoulders as I held on while ecstacy barrelled through me. I felt his cock twitch inside of me as he shouted my name, and then he leant his head against mine as we took a moment to come back to ourselves, before placing me gently on the ground, not releasing me until he knew that I was stable.

He turned to grab my vanilla scented body wash, giving me the perfect view of his muscled back and dimpled ass.

Lifting my gaze, I hesitated on his shoulder.

"Shit," I hissed, standing on my tiptoes to touch the deep scratches that were bleeding slightly. "Why didn't you say anything?" I demanded.

"Because I didn't mind, and I didn't want you to stop," he said, turning around to face me.

"But I hurt you," I implored.

"Aria," he sighed, "it takes a lot more than some nail gouges to hurt me. I liked seeing you like that, knowing that I made you that wild, that it was *me* you lost control with."

I sighed in defeat, looking up at him through the droplets or water pouring down between us.

"What now?" I asked, hating that my question would ruin this moment, but now that I was feeling less unhinged, I needed to know where Ajax and I stood. I certainly did not want a relationship with this man - he was a Society asshole, but did that mean we went back to being enemies? Did we ignore each other completely? Or were we once again aiming for *civility?*

"Now, we go and eat some pizza and watch some more of that series you had on, and then," he spoke carefully, rubbing the soapy sponge against my shoulders in a soothing, circular motion, staring at me intently, "I'm going to fuck you again, so that come tomorrow, you won't be able to *sit* without thinking about me."

I blushed furiously, casting my eyes on the ground.

His laughter eased the tension that had coiled within and I glanced back up at him.

"We *can't* do this," I implored, willing him to see what I was trying to communicate with my eyes.

"We'll just be discreet," he offered with an infuriating grin.

"You mean we'll *hide,"* I countered.

His eyes flared in anger, "Do you *want* The Society to find out about us?" He narrowed his gaze at me, "because if you do, then by all means march down the hallway and shout it from the rooftops, but be prepared for the consequences of your actions, because as soon as they discover that this thing between is has sparked into the sexual realm, they will be putting us forward for the fucking breeding programme."

I blinked in surprise at him.

"Yes," he spat, "I'm a good soldier up to a point, but there are some aspects of my life that *I* would like to remain in control over."

I breathed through my whirling thoughts.

"So we remain discreet?" I asked.

I watched the tension ease in his face, as if he may have been worried that I would use his big confession against him somehow. In the end, we were all trying to run from the weight of expectations that The Society placed upon us.

"Yeah," he sounded gruff, "we remain discreet."

"And after summer?" I asked quietly, needing to know that he would release me once our time had been served.

"Then we enter back into the real world, with none the wiser, and carry on with our separate lives."

Relief coursed through me.

"Fine," I agreed.

"Fine?"

"Yes," I blew out, "I'm not exactly lining up to be entered into the breeding programme," I admitted.

He offered me a tight smile.

"Should we shake on it?" I asked, only half-joking.

His laughter was unexpected, as he stepped forward and brought his lips to mine.

"You and I?" He whispered against my lips, "we don't shake on things. We fuck."

It was my turn to laugh.

Ajax dried off, leaving me to muddle through my own thoughts as I dressed.

I walked out wearing a sheer black babydoll slip, knowing full well that I was playing with fire.

"What?" I asked innocently as Ajax watched me. "This is my sleep wear."

"Fucking hell," he muttered, turning on the show.

It was domestic, sitting on my bed with Ajax, eating pizza and watching series, knowing that we would have sex at least one more time before the morning.

He tracked my movements, watching each bite of food I ate intently. And when he was satisfied that I had in fact eaten, he pounced, flipping me onto my knees and taking me from behind. It was the same way Raul had had me earlier, but as Ajax slid in and out of me, I realised that there was no comparison. I screamed his name as I climaxed on his cock, with him collapsing on top of me as he found his release shortly after mine.

Completely sated and unable to move, Ajax lifted me, placing me under the covers. He switched the series off and slid in next to me as I drifted in and out of a sleepy, satisfied haze.

"I'm sleeping here from now onwards," he said matter-of-factly.

Sleep engulfed me before I could even reply.

In the darkness of the bedroom, sometime in the middle of the night, Ajax and I found each other, joining fiercely between clinging, scratching, and biting. I screamed in pleasure into the pillow as Ajax brought me to release over and over again.

By the time the morning light had started filtering through, Ajax was already forming lazy patterns with his fingers along my spine. It was as if we could not get enough of each other. As if we needed to experience as much of each other as possible before we braved the outside world once more.

Knowing where his hands would ultimately end up, I shifted, pinning him with my own weight, sliding my body down his chest to finally grip him by the base.

He cocked an eyebrow in response to my exploration, and *because* of his self assuredness, I placed my lips around his head and sucked him in deep.

His fingers thread themselves into my hair, and I allowed him to push me deeper, taking more of him in my mouth. I flicked him with my tongue, watching his cock jerk in response, before once more taking him as deep as I could go. Because he was so big, there was still a lot of space at the base of his cock, and so I worked him with my hands from the bottom, and my mouth from the top.

His hips thrust up, pushing him deeper, and I felt his muscles quiver and tense beneath me, which only made me work harder.

He fisted my hair, making a garbled sound as he tried to form words. I liked seeing him this unhinged.

His cock jerked in my mouth, flooding my senses with the salty taste that was all Ajax. I swallowed him all down before releasing him from my mouth.

"Good morning!" I said, sounding chipper.

"That was… fuck," Ajax said.

"I'm going to make us coffee," I said, sliding out the bed, giving him a few moments to collect himself.

I felt him slide up behind me as I waited for the coffee mugs to fill, his hand slipping beneath my sheer slip.

"I seem to be indebted to you, Miss O'Luc," he whispered seductively in my ear.

I groaned in response, grinding back against him.

Before there was time for us to even spring apart, the front door swung open, Joshua standing in the doorway holding a tray of donuts.

"When did this happen?" Josh walked in grinning.

"How are you in our suite?" I asked, perplexed.

"I gave him a key," Ajax offered.

"You gave him a key?" I repeated.

He flashed an apologetic smile at me before turning towards Josh.

"We are keeping it discreet," he offered with a tight smile.

"Well, I'm not going to say a word. The two of you will be set up in the breeding programme given half the chance," Joshua confirmed, "I mean, Ajax, your dad has been on you for ages about settling down, so this thing between you two needs to be kept quiet."

I absorbed that information, schooling my face into a blank expression.

"Not that you're not lovely, Aria," Joshua said to me.

"I'm not offended," I reassured them both.

"Good," he said, laying the donuts on the kitchen counter.

Ajax shifted in front of me, blocking my view, and it took me a minute to realise that he was shielding me from Joshua because I was still in my sheer slip.

"I'm going to change," I muttered, slipping away from the two of them and heading towards the bedroom.

"Nice ass!" Joshua called out after me.

Naturally, I flipped him off.

CHAPTER NINETEEN : A GAME OF PRETEND

Like clockwork, our morning began in the basement, where O'Grady would be teaching us some more intimate hand-to-hand combat techniques.

Ajax and Joshua would be in the ring - according to both of them, it was how they liked to warm up for the day - while I would join the rest of the candidates with O'Grady.

"Are you okay?" Raquel took her position next to me. "We missed you yesterday."

"Assignment," I nodded. I did not miss the flicker of concern creep across her face.

I shook it off and got myself into position, lest O'Grady kick my ass for slacking off.

Was I really here only yesterday morning? It seemed like a lifetime. A lot had changed... and nothing had changed, because I was still here, still part of The Society. I flicked my gaze behind me to find Ajax's eyes planted firmly on mine, as if he knew the things plaguing my mind.

Suddenly under his gaze, I was more aware of O' Grady's hands that lingered at my waist, and the stare that he held for a beat too long.

While Ajax and I hadn't promised each other anything, I got the distinct impression that he wasn't the sharing type. Since I enjoyed pushing boundaries, I may have lent into O'Grady's hands on my waist - just slightly - which caused a flicker of surprise to appear on his face for a milli-second, but I saw it. Because I wanted to see what Ajax would do *and* because I needed to see if Ajax was just simply another level of control within The Society - or if he was something else entirely.

"You are playing with fire," Raquel said, noticing Ajax's scathing stares in our direction.

"I don't know what you're talking about," I smiled blandly.

She laughed darkly. I cast my glance back towards Ajax as unease settled within me. He narrowed his gaze at me. Yeah, he and I would be talking.

As our session with O'Grady ended, I two-stepped it back to our suite, knowing that Ajax would need more time to get out of the ring.

I suddenly wasn't feeling so confident in pushing these boundaries. I didn't know what Ajax would do, but I knew that he wasn't happy.

He burst into the suite a few minutes after I did. I swallowed, staring at his imposing figure as he stalked towards me.

"What the fuck are you playing at, Aria?"

I swallowed, refusing to cower in response, instead I jutted my chin out. "We don't owe each other anything."

He growled, and in two swift strides, he was before me, pushing me against the wall, caging me in with all of his senses.

"When you're in *my* bed," he growled into my ear, his breath hitting my neck, sending shivers across my skin, "you're *only* in my bed."

My eyes fluttered shut at the sensation of lips almost touching my neck, and I had to fight for the control to respond fairly - evenly - to him. Because he wasn't playing fair.

"That's not fair." My impetulance was undermined by the breathy tenor of my voice.

"Oh?" He asked, his hand making slow, languid movements, just beneath my shirt, grazing my stomach with the back of his knuckles.

"You leave the compound regularly for your... *extracurricular* activities," my breathing was becoming harder.

"And why would I want to leave the compound when you're in my bed?"

I fought the urge to smile.

"*My* bed," I responded, not quite willing to let him win this power struggle.

"*Our* bed," he growled, his hand finally sliding all the way beneath my shirt, slipping underneath my bra.

"What does that mean?" I panted, biting down on my lip as my nipples hardened in response to his calloused palm as it slid across my breast.

"I don't share," he spoke low and seductively, just before he kissed my neck, right where my pulse jumped in response to his.

Before I lost myself completely to him and the moment, I splayed a hand across his chest, pushing back slightly.

He released me, his gaze seeking out my own.

"Neither do I," I said, holding his gaze.

He gave the slightest dip of his chin in acknowledgement, and then his lips crashed into mine, demanding and relentless in its desire.

Breaking the kiss, he spun me around, placing both of my hands on the wall. He slid my pants down, allowing them to rest at the ankles, creating resistance each time I tried to further part my thighs.

My breasts brushed against the wall, creating a delicious type of friction as he slid into my entrance slowly.

I groaned loudly, needing to feel more of him. I slid back against him until his entire length was inside of me.

The pace he set was punishing, the restrictive clothing only adding to the heat of it all.

All I could do was brace myself against the wall as I took everything Ajax was offering. As his pounding grew more frantic - more wild - he slid his fingers between my legs, working my clit in a toe-curling manner.

His name flew off of my lips as I shattered around him, my orgasm consuming in its strength. Ajax came at the same time.

I pressed my forehead against the wall, panting as I allowed my mind to reacquaint itself with my body.

Ajax pressed a light kiss against my spine before he pulled away.

"Shower?" He murmured.

I nodded, slipping off my clothing, allowing him to lead the way towards the bathroom.

What had I just agreed to? But it was more than that, because I didn't just simply agree - I had contributed, holding my own in that conversation. And now? Now I had an intimate level of exclusivity with Ajax SinClaire.

And that thought both thrilled and terrified me.

Ajax was attentive in the shower, shampooing my hair in a way that sent warmth shooting to my core. And when my breathing became uneven, he knelt before me, hoisting my leg on his shoulder, and began licking and nipping my sex with his tongue.

He had me panting and calling his name as if he were the person who would answer my prayers. And when his tongue slid inside me, moving in quick thrusts, I gripped his shoulders, shaking and quivering as my orgasm rocked through me.

We took our seats at our respective separate tables at lunch. I tried to keep up with the conversations of Mack and Raquel, and it took all my willpower to stop my gaze from darting towards Ajax. The only measure of contentment I had was that Ajax was probably fighting the same urge himself.

As if confirming that theory, Josh's gaze flicked towards us. I grinned at him knowingly.

And so, the game of pretend was in motion.

We ate dinner at Joe's where Ajax sat in his usual booth, content to enjoy his evening in the same vicinity as one another, but separated and shielded from the prying eyes of The Society. I did not miss the lingering looks and light 'accidental' touches when we passed one another.

By the time we had both retired for the evening, it was an explosion of ripping clothes and fierce need. *Later*, when we weren't quite so frenzied, we would enjoy each other at a steadier pace. But that initial joining after spending the day apart was animalistic, and I loved every thick inch of it.

The next few weeks were filled with the game of pretend, with each of us reiterating how we despised the other. In order to not rouse suspicion, Ajax left the compound a few times, leaving everyone to believe that he was meeting a woman off site. But I knew that he was actually sitting at the cinema, biding his time to come back and fuck me.

Those were the nights I made him work for it the most.

It didn't matter what happened during the day, come sundown, we were always tangled up in one another. The sex was hard, fast and brutal - all the ways that I liked it.

Joshua had taken to acting out vomiting sounds each time he saw us together, but honestly - I didn't care. We were insatiable, and if I were being completely honest with myself, it had also been the best sex of my life.

True to his possessive nature, Ajax took it upon himself to teach me combat training, knife skills and the various ways of handling a firearm. While I didn't hate the additional one-on-one time with Ajax, because these lessons took place in the basement, we often drew a crowd, which meant we had to be extra-careful when it came to groping and touching.

These lessons only heightened our need for one another, with one night culminating in Ajax pushing me deep into a booth at the shooting range as the lights of the basement dimmed for the night.

Boosting me onto the counter, he pulled my thighs towards the edge, until it was only him that was holding me stable. And then he thrust into me. And in. And in. Consuming me until my walls were clenching around him as I screamed out his name, not caring in that moment who heard us. His hand splayed against the wall as he came inside of me in a fast, jerking motion.

He held onto me until my legs stopped quivering and my heart stopped racing, and when we were done, he linked his fingers with mine and guided me out of the shooting range, into the darkness of the basement.

And in between all the hardness and passion, there were soft moments, too. Moments where he became more than just the asshole who just so happened to give me multiple orgasms in one session.

Pizza and series became a standard event in our suite, and I learnt that Ajax was capable of not being an asshole all of the time. He had a sharp sense of humour and unrivalled wit, challenging me at every turn.

He loved horror and action packed shows, whereas I enjoyed some light romance, or dramatic shows that contained tons of nude scenes. In the end, we would always compromise on some sort of comedic series where we both contribute to our running commentary during the entire thing.

He had been *working* for The Society since he was fifteen - the weight of his family's expectations heavy across his brow. His mother was a standard copy and past Society woman, and his father was a man who was only content at the realm of power - in this case, one of the heads within The Society.

And when our conversation turned towards The Society, behind the closed doors of our suite, I heard the underlying bitterness of his responses, and I understood that he too was desperate to not be controlled, yet had simply resigned himself to the fact that there was no way out for him - for us.

My heart ached for the fifteen-year-old boy he once was, who was sent to The Society to be trained in weaponry and combat so that he could bring honour to his family by 'serving earlier'. For the boy who had a love for sports, but was never allowed to pursue it because it did not align with his family's expectations for him. And for the boy who knew that he had no shot at a real relationship, because in the end, The Society would determine who he should settle down with for breeding purposes.

And, as I understood it, if we were to compare lineage and pedigrees, he would be of the highest form, making his breeding match all the more scrutinised.

CHAPTER TWENTY : PLAYING THE HERO

The third phase of the assignment - which was actually saving those girls, took ages to plan and strategize - well, at least in my mind, it did. I somehow kept expecting it to happen pretty much overnight, and to be fair, the first two experiences I had had within this assignment were fast moving, occurring within days of one another.

But that is not what happened. Due to those miniscule camera feeds that Ajax had planted, The Society had an uninterrupted view of what was happening at the warehouse - at least within the customer areas. Based on this, The Society were able to determine how the girls were, who was working in rotation, and if anyone was injured.

Ajax and I attended numerous planning and strategizing meetings, where I came to understand that before going to save them, we needed to set up a safe house to move them to within close proximity of the warehouse. Transport vans needed to be attended, as well as the seemingly never-ending debate of *where* these vans should be stationed prior to saving them. Benson and Ajax seemed to be unable to agree on any detail, and even I knew that something deeper was brewing.

Doctors, therapists and a 'handler', all needed to be on standby at the safe house for when we delivered the girls there. Clothing and toiletries needed to be stocked up on.

And then, there was the actual planning of how we would be getting them out.

It wasn't an eloquent plan - not by a long shot. In fact, it mostly consisted of The Society swarming the warehouse and simply taking the girls.

Ajax and I were both required to be there for the heist, and it frightened me that I wasn't more frightened. In fact, with Ajax next to me, I felt exhilarated.

"Perhaps the way in should be with you returning Aria to them? Stating that she wasn't what you expected and that you'd like to renegotiate... something along those lines?" Benson proposed.

"No," Ajax snapped.

"No?" Benson queried, almost mockingly.

It took everything within me to not sink into my chair and act guilty.

"Must every person debase themselves entirely in order for The Society to achieve what they wish?" He seethed.

"I suppose we could just stick to the plan - although it will, no doubt, be far messier," Benson drawled. "Aria dear, which would you prefer?"

I wanted the Earth to swallow me whole as Ajax, Benson, Sarah and a few other Society members all looked at me, waiting for my response.

"I, ah, would prefer not to be a brothel prostitute?" My nerves made me end my sentence as if it were a question, but at least I had said it.

Benson glanced back at Ajax. "Fine," he grumbled. And suddenly we were back to strategizing a full on, guns blazing kind of heist.

Even with all the extra one-on-one training from Ajax - and even I had to admit that the man could hold his own in a fight - I was so ill prepared to be part of this mission. It was frightening.

Our team assembled in a private room in the basement, fitting our armoured vests on, strapping in our knives and arming ourselves to the teeth with all sorts of guns and weaponry. Ajax walked towards me to double check my armour, his gaze strong and heavy upon mine.

"Stay close to me, okay?" He spoke softly, the thread of worry evident within his voice.

"Yeah, okay," I nodded. I wasn't an idiot. I knew that Ajax would keep me safe.

He bent down, sliding a blue knife into the intricate holder that was strapped to my thigh. I held in my breath as his fingertips grazed my leg. Flashes from the night before rolled unbidden through my mind, reminding me exactly how skilled he was with those fingers.

"How many of these types of operations have you done?" I asked, in a bid to distract myself from where my traitorous thoughts had turned.

He turned his head towards mine, looking up at me from next to my thigh.

"Too many," his voice was low and gruff, as if his thoughts had followed mine, casting up images of the two of us tangled together.

Before I was ready, we were moving out with The Society's version of a swat team. My palms became clammy, and I remained next to Ajax as we all climbed into a large white van.

He squeezed my thigh once in reassurance, and then we were off and all I could do was remind myself to breathe.

It felt as if it were only a few moments had passed as our van pulled into the gravelly lot of the warehouse. The door slid open and our swat team poured out. My body seemed to be working on autopilot, with my legs carrying me after the crowd. I ducked with military precision as we were met with a spray of gunfire coming from the front of the warehouse. As if all the training I had done had kicked in on some instinctive level, I did not even have the time to feel gratitude, instead I released my firearm and opened fire back at them.

I vaguely heard Ajax bark a laugh and yell, "that's my girl," but I could not focus on him. Not now.

Once the gunfire ceased, we were moving, the front door standing wide open.

The open plan chamber was eerily quiet and empty, those brightly coloured cushions now scattered along the floor.

Gunfire sounded to our left, with one of ours returning it with a few shots before the enemy was silenced.

Working in unison, we split up in groups, Ajax and I, along with a few others, walking towards the long passage where I was held captive.

The hallway was shrouded in darkness, causing unease to flicker through me. Which was ridiculous, because we were in the middle of a heist. Nothing about this should have been easy.

Someone in our team kicked in the first door leading off the hallway. We were only met with darkness and silence. It was empty.

The next door where the girl who had been drugged was kept provided an empty bed and no movement. Empty.

Bullets hailed down upon us as we kicked the third door open. The stock room filled with boxes of ammunition was being protected by Samuele. He had a manic gleam in his eye as he screamed a slew of unintelligible insults at us while swinging his rifle back and forth, his finger never lifting off the trigger.

I heard someone from our team go down with a loud "ooof" and a thud, but we did not have the luxury of time. We could not stop and check him over.

Instead, Ajax pushed me behind him and with two precise shots, took Samuele down with a bullet between his eyes.

His body swayed slightly before he collapsed to the ground. His last insult still ringing in my ears.

"Society trash."

He knew exactly who we were.

Ajax's hand found its way to the small of my back, guiding me forward while another man shielded us from the front. I understood a minute too late what he was doing as I tried to turn back to look at the man who had fallen - the one who was ours. He pushed me forward, not giving me an inch. And I knew then that the man behind me did not make it and that even in this moment, even when we had nothing more to give than what The Society allowed us, that Ajax was protecting me.

So I gave him that. I kept my head forward and allowed him to guide me along until we reached the room at the end of the hallway.

Manuela stood fiercely, a pistol in her hand, as the girls crowded behind her, eyes widened with fear.

"You are pathetic," she screamed at us, "you come in here to take them away from us just so you can use them for your own purposes - as if you and your fucking Society are somehow better than us," she hissed.

And if the situation wasn't so fucked up, I may have viewed her as a lioness defending her cubs. But she was a human trafficker, and she was only defending her income - nothing more.

She fired her pistol towards us, Ajax expertly pushing us out the way in the nick of time.

It wasn't a fair fight, not in the least. But we were not here to be fair, we were here to offer these women freedom.

A hail of bullets rained down upon her, punching holes in her abdomen and chest. Her body seemed to convulse with each bullet it absorbed. Blood leaked from her mouth as she said, "Soldero will never let this stand." And then she was gone.

Our team got to ushering the girls out, whispered words of reassurance to get them moving to safety. I flicked over their faces, mentally categorising each one.

"Where is Andrea?" I asked.

No one answered me, in fact, one girl deliberately looked at the ground, avoiding my question - or, perhaps avoiding conversation and contact after everything she had endured.

"Where is Andrea?" I repeated the question, louder this time.

A blonde girl shook her head, her eyes filled with sadness.

"What happened?" I demanded.

"She went too far and angered Raul," another girl offered.

The floor felt as if it had been ripped out from under me as my head swam. We were too late. We were too late and had allowed Andrea to be killed at the hands of that monster.

"Where is Raul?" I asked, suddenly realising that I had not seen him in the warehouse.

"From what we can gleam, he was sent out on another job for Soldero," someone on our team provided.

Ajax grabbed my shaking hand, rubbing soothing strikes against my skin to calm me. I was disgusted and furious and heartbroken. I was a kaleidoscope of emotions. But I couldn't give myself over to them, not here at least, and so I shouldered an injured girl and guided her outside and into the van.

The girls were cold and frightened - all dressed in scraps of material that barely covered anything.

I grabbed two large blankets out of the car and laid it across them as best I could before we drove them to the safe house.

The safe house was just another warehouse, and I tried to suppress the shiver that ran through me at how similar this place was to Soldero's.

Once we walked inside, I saw that the layout was different. Large rooms had been converted into dormitories, with beds lining the walls. Clothing had been laid out on each. A small sitting room had been set up, with navy leather couches and a TV running episodes of The Kardashians.

Some of the girls started crying, while others blinked in shock, as if they were waiting for something terrible to occur - not quite trusting the situation.

Dr. Leila Oswaldo stepped forward, welcoming the girls with a warm smile. I immediately felt better seeing her there. She explained that she wanted to conduct medical exams on each of them, so that she could provide them with the healthcare that they needed. Some of them blatantly refused - not wanting any form of contact. My heart squeezed painfully in my chest as I wondered at the horrors that had been inflicted upon them.

Pizza and burgers were brought out for them, and soon the occasional sound of laughter could be heard - as if they finally understood that they were in fact free; even if that laughter sounded foreign after everything they had endured.

CHAPTER TWENTY-ONE : SO THIS IS GOODBYE

When we were finally alone, Ajax turned to me and asked, "Are you okay?"

I looked at him, unable to find it within myself to lie - to hold up that carefully learnt front that I boasted to the world, "No," I said, "I am not okay."

To his credit, Ajax didn't try to tell me not to worry about it, or that it would all be okay.

He simply led me into the bathroom and began filling the tub, dumping far too much of my expensive bath salts into the bubbling water. But even so, I could not bring myself to berate him. Not in this moment. Not now. Not when I was feeling so raw.

As I sank beneath the water, I felt a wave of anguish coat my tongue, watching the water ebb and flow around me.

Ajax sat in silence next to the tub, offering me his strength through the simple act of his presence, in a way that I never knew I needed.

The sobs racked through my body in waves as I grieved for the loss of Andrea - for the belief that I had debased myself to *save* her and somehow still failed.

Ajax didn't say a word. He simply grabbed the sponge and washed my back as I sobbed, needing some form of release. He lightly kissed my head, finally whispering, "You're okay," and, "I've got you."

When all the sobs had been racked from my body, I sat in the now lukewarm water, numb and exhausted in a way that I had never before experienced.

Ajax scooped me out of the water, wrapping me in a white towel. Even though it was soft, the coarseness of the material felt right against my sensitive skin, as if everything was too overwhelming somehow.

Depositing me on the bed, he put on our series and simply allowed me to not be okay. He commented on the parts that required commentary, and ordered food in when it was time to eat, but mostly he was just there.

It's funny. At the beginning of my servitude, I had been dreading coming here. Dreading the noose around my neck that The Society seemed to tighten with each movement - each stepping stone of my life, and yet as the days trickled by, I found myself wanting to slow down time just so I could be here a little bit longer.

I knew that it was because of Ajax. I knew that I had allowed him to crawl under my skin. I also knew that I was a fucking idiot, because he was still an asshole.

I grew accustomed to him being there, making me coffee in the morning, picking up another jar of my favourite bath salts during one of his trips to town, and knowing exactly what my favourites were off our take out menu. This kind of domesticity was, well, *nice.*

"I'm so glad they fixed the shower head from the last time I was here," he said, stepping into the bedroom dressed in a tux.

I looked at him through the full-length mirror as I adjusted my earrings - tear drop diamonds to match the shimmering dress that clung to every curve of my body.

"What do you mean?" I asked.

He made a low sound in the back of his throat and I couldn't tell if it was because of my outfit or because of what he had just said.

I tracked his line of sight, watching his gaze drift lower with each second.

I cleared my throat, attempting to get the conversation back on course. I *knew* that look, and if I gave him even the remotest impression that I was entertaining that thought, I would be pinned beneath him in a heartbeat. And we really needed to get to The Society's farewell function.

"I used to stay in this suite every time I came here," he admitted sheepishly, his gaze flicking back towards my face.

"Really?" I was surprised. "Why did they put me here then?"

He grunted noncommittally, "I may have given the impression that I would never get involved with someone from The Society, and I think this was my father's way of nudging me into a different way of thinking."

"And," I swallowed my nerves, "Did it work?"

His eyes shuttered and a look of sadness encompassed him so fully that my heart cracked at what he was about to say.

"No, not really," he said, "it can't, because I refuse to partake in their breeding programme, to be *used* in the way where any child I have will be subjected to this life."

I understood. I wish I didn't, but I did. And even though my heart was cracking, I offered him a sad smile and said, "That's why you were having all those dates offside?"

He grimaced, "Yeah," rubbing the back of his neck, "I chose all the girls that I knew they wouldn't approve of - just to be safe."

We stood in silence, allowing all those unsaid things to linger in the air.

As I pulled out a diamond necklace, Ajax stepped forward.

"Allow me."

His touch was featherlight, as if he too knew that one lingering touch or smoldering look and we wouldn't be leaving this room. His breath skittered along my back when he was done as he leaned forward and said, "I'm going to be having one hell of a time trying to *not* look at you in this."

The gold dress was provocative, not only because of how skintight it was but also because of the cleavage it displayed and the long slit that ran up to my thigh. The beading over the dress only served to make it shimmer, ensuring that it was a showstopper in the truest sense of the word.

Ajax entered before me, as he was expected to present with the other instructors, while I followed a cool thirty minutes behind.

The cafeteria had been converted into something spectacular for the evening. Golden lights had been weaved in between the greenery that was hanging from the ceiling.

The wrought-iron tables had been replaced with ones that were much larger, wooden, and equally round.

The night held a nostalgic sort of energy to it, the kind that I imagined would be associated with the last night of summer camp. Although I had never been allowed to attend, I felt as if it were a plausible guess.

Raquel wore a deep garnet dress with a high collar and severe neckline that plunged to just above her belly button. She looked simultaneously striking and intimidating. Champagne flutes did the rounds, and within the buzz of people, I felt unsettled.

Mack had a scowl plastered across his face the entire evening, and I didn't have to be a neurosurgeon to know that it had to do with Marissa, sitting two tables behind us, casting furtive glances in his direction.

Needing to rid myself from some of the tension, I walked across to the newly erected bar that was propped against the vine-covered wall.

"Bourbon, please," the voice next to me spoke.

I found myself face to face with Benson.

I flashed him a tight smile, my stomach plummeting with nerves. Something about the man set me on edge, and the bits and pieces that Ajax had shared about his childhood did not exactly paint him as a model parent.

"Mr. SinClaire," I acknowledged politely.

"Ah, Aria," he greeted me with a warm smile, "I hope your experience with us exceeded expectations, although I am sorry to see that you and Ajax did not get along nearly as half as well as I had hoped."

The barkeep placed my glass on the table, and I gripped the stem of my champagne flute steadily, sipping on it before I replied. *Thank god he did not know.* That was the only thought that was running through my mind as I politely responded, "It has definitely been enlightening."

He merely nodded, releasing me from the awkwardness of it all.

I felt Ajax's gaze on me as I walked away, using all of my willpower to not look over at him and reassure him that nothing nefarious was said or promised.

As the party branched out in full swing, Raquel made her way to the dancefloor, dragging both Mack and myself with her.

"I will not let our last memory of our time here be of you two moping at the table," she admonished.

Her body moved as if the beat was the very air she breathed. Raquel was magnificent. She was funny, talented and raw. And, I was so happy to have met her. She filled the void that Natalia had left - not in the same way, but in a way that allowed me to open up and *live*.

Mack moved to the beat, throwing shot back after shot, and it made me think that he and I had come full circle.

Joshua's gaze was on Raquel the entire night, and for once, her gaze did not seek his out. She simply lived as if she did not care that he was watching, and I envied that.

The night ended with the three of us belting out the lyrics to The Kids Aren't Alright by The Offspring, and I wondered if each of our assignments had left us all feeling a little too raw - a little *too* changed. As if after this experience, we would somehow be unable to fit back into society.

We split up to our respective rooms, promising to stay in touch and see each other. I hoped we would keep those promises, but I also knew that the real world had a way of encroaching on dreams and skewered promises.

Ajax wasn't in our suite by the time I stumbled in, which wasn't all that surprising considering I had last seen him at the bar with Paul and Josh, going through a line of shot glasses.

The sheets felt cold, and the bed somehow too big without him, and I hated myself for allowing myself to feel this way - for being the type of girl that grew giddy for a man. With those thoughts simmering in my mind, I drifted off to sleep.

A warm body that smelled heavily of whisky was pressed against me, an arm thrown around my waist. I pressed back within his firmness and something within my chest eased slightly as I drifted back to sleep.

The blaring of an alarm sounded, urging us to get up and *leave*. I cracked one eye open and was greeted by the cool dimness of the early morning filtering through the curtains. The sun hadn't even risen yet.

Ajax swore, banging the alarm clock off, before his hand made its way back to my waist.

"Why are we awake at this time?" I grumbled.

"Because I have the red-eye flight to catch," he whispered back at me.

Suddenly, the thing I had been trying to keep at bay was here, and I didn't know how I felt about that.

Turning in his arms, I kissed him slowly, allowing my tongue to explore and dance with his. And when he moved over me, it was unhurried, as if he too were trying to delay the inevitable.

Ajax slid his body against mine, building up the tension through slow, teasing touches.

When he finally slid into me, he remained close, moving inside me in a way that spoke of longing. Interlacing his fingers with mine, he moved languidly, and the slowness and care of his movements created a new sensation entirely.

My back arched off the mattress, my soft moans filling the bedroom as exquisite euphoria barrelled down my spine as I climaxed. Ajax's lips met mine, devouring my sounds.

He exploded in me soon after, and I simply wrapped my legs around him and held him through it.

Lying in bed, sated with Ajax's hands tracing light patterns against my skin, I think I may have hated time.

When he could no longer linger and made to leave the bed, I wrapped my legs around his waist and pulled him back towards me. He kissed me deeply, and I wanted so desperately for this to be *real*.

Pulling away, he lay his forehead against mine and whispered, "Bye Aria."

And then he was gone. Bags somehow packed the night before - as if he knew this moment would be impossible.

CHAPTER TWENTY-TWO :
SAXON AND SAXON

Saxon and Saxon was exactly what you would expect from a large, corporate publishing house that was controlled by The Society.

Upon arrival, I was offered a private office with large swinging glass doors that gave me an unhindered view of the open plan office, and it showcased me to them in return.

Even I could see the ridiculousness of the situation. I was a graduate straight out of university, being given a private office, whilst many here had been part of the firm for years and were still stuck in their cubicles outside my door.

As if the situation wasn't ludicrous as it was, a young blonde woman arrived at my office, announcing herself as my assistant. Her name was Jane and I was fairly certain that she had more experience in this industry than I had.

I couldn't sink into my chair and acknowledge that I was undeserving of such privileges, because that would undermine The Society. So I sat, smiled politely, shuffled papers around on my desk and pretended to know what I was doing.

The flight here had been a flurry of motion, where everything seemed to move at an incredible pace. It helped though. The busy part ensured that I couldn't think about Ajax - because there simply wasn't time. That had been my modus of operandi, but as I sat, removed from everyone in their cubicles, isolated and alone, I knew that I wouldn't be able to keep it up.

The days bled into one another; the nights being the worst. I didn't *want* to miss him, but my body hadn't seemed to get that memo, and when I woke sweat slicked from yet another dream about him, I eventually glided my fingers into myself expertly.

I wondered what he was doing, how his business was going and if he was back to swiping right for all those non-Society girls. That last thought turned my stomach into knots as the green eyes of jealousy reared its ugly head.

We did not owe each other anything, and he had made his stance on sustaining a relationship with someone who was part of The Society quite clear. And if I examined my thoughts rationally, I knew that I didn't want to be serving The Society indefinitely. But I did want him - that I could no longer deny.

I survived my first week at Saxon and Saxon, and honestly, even if I did absolutely nothing all day, they wouldn't fire me, because I was part of The Society. There was something depressing about working towards something but never truly given the opportunity to earn it, simply because it is handed to you anyway. It made you doubt your value as a person and whether you had any skill set to offer the world at all.

I spent the first weekend by myself in over three months, curled up on the couch, watching reruns of the old series. I couldn't bring myself to watch *How I Met Your Mother*, not without him, anyway.

Somewhere along the line, I had allowed Ajax SinClaire to creep beneath my skin, and in those wallowing, pitiful moments, I hated him. I hated him for the asshole that he was, because he got me to see him for more than just the surface prick he was, and when I began falling a little in love with him, he left.

Natalia wasn't back yet, sending me some cryptic messages about extending her vacation and taking ownership of her life - so I couldn't even wallow with her.

Holed up on my couch, I allowed myself to grieve, refusing to shower for two days, only content to leave the comfort of my couch for food delivery.

I was a mess, but I was allowing myself the weekend before I had to pull myself together. It rained the entire weekend, making me wonder if it wasn't cleansing in some way - washing away the hold that Ajax and all the memories of him had on me.

By the time Monday rolled around, I showered, dressed and acted like a functioning adult who contributed to the economy - even if that was the furthest thing from how I truly felt.

The office was abuzz as I walked through the doors, everyone talking about the news that had broken over the weekend and what such a power play could mean. Of course, because I had been glued to my sofa, feeling sorry for myself for the entire weekend, I had no idea what they were talking about. So I simply kept my head down and smiled when necessary.

My office became a reprieve from the madness, but it did not take me long to see what had everyone giddy with excitement.

There, on the front page of the New York Times, was the story of the season. Ajax SinClaire had welcomed Joshua Penn (heir to the founders of Penn University) as the Vice President of Molton Tech. The article waxed on lyrically about what Josh would bring to the table, labelling the two a 'formidable' pair.

I folded the newspaper neatly and placed it on the edge of my desk, not wanting to read any further.

Jane glided in, announcing that the PR firm that we had partnered with to arrange a few book tours had arrived, and that the meeting was set to begin shortly.

Thank you Jane, who was more competent than I was in so many aspects.

Sighing, I lifted the book portfolio and followed after Jane as she led me to one of the many meeting rooms Saxon and Saxon boasted.

"Well, you look like shit," a female voice drawled.

I snapped my head up to find Raquel lounging at the table, and I had never been more relieved to see a member of The Society.

"What are you doing in my meeting?" I laughed back.

"Haven't you heard?" She raised her eyebrows suggestively. "I'm the new representative for Satin Public Relations.

My answering grin was one filled with joy. Because despite Raquel's wayward ways, I still considered her a friend.

Raquel and I began plotting and planning a national book tour, the hours shuttling away slowly.

"Want to grab a drink?" She smirked at me, and for the first time in a week, I felt lighter.

O' Mally's was exactly the way I had remembered it - loud and obtuse.

"This was your local?" Raquel scrunched up her nose in distaste.

"Come on," I rolled my eyes, dragging her to the bar.

"Look what the cat dragged in," Jack bantered from behind the bar.

"Hello, Jack," I smiled, "we need to celebrate this fine woman next to me, and her mad book tour planning skills, so line them up."

Jack did as he was told. My praise for Raquel going straight over his head.

We danced and drank and flirted up a storm, and I threw myself into those activities wholeheartedly, in an attempt to simply forget Ajax and the way he knew how to work my body better than I did.

As we stumbled into a booth, giggling and gasping for air, Raquel leant across the table, her gaze focused on mine.

"Ajax is an asshole," she slurred.

My stomach sank as I gave her a sad smile and shrugged. "How did you know?"

Immediately, she began shaking her head, "I came up to your suite one morning and heard you two," she giggled.

Suddenly, I was blushing furiously - no wonder Joshua was always smirking at us.

"Don't worry, only Josh and I know," she said - as if that were supposed to be reassuring.

"You and Josh discussed us?" I hissed.

"Relax," she rolled her eyes, "it came up when we went to the basement to train one evening and you two were there."

"Oh God," I groaned, covering my face in embarrassment as I sent a prayer up to the heavens that she left *before* Ajax had his way with me in the shooting range.

She laughed teasingly, which did absolutely nothing to calm my nerves.

"We left before anything serious went down, but the chemistry between the two of you was fucking tangible."

I groaned, slumping down, resting my head on the sticky surface of the table.

"Was the sex at least good?" Raquel pestered.

I glared up at her in reply.

"Obviously it was," she laughed, playing with her straw in her drink, "otherwise you wouldn't look like your grandmother died."

"I do not look *that* bad," I countered, snapping my head up off the table.

"To people who don't know you - sure, you don't look bad, you're still a knockout, but I saw you when you were carefree and having fun, and you do not look like that person."

"I hate you," I glared at her.

Her responding chuckle only aggregated me further.

"What about you and Josh?" I asked, needing to change the topic.

"We want different things," She shrugged nonchalantly.

"Meaning?"

"Meaning that he wants a wife and children, and I… don't."

"Why not?" I asked. I knew that she had no interest in becoming someone's wife, but I would keep asking if it kept the questions about Ajax and I at bay.

"Why don't I want a wife?" She spoke with mischief gleaming in her eye.

"Raquel," I warned.

"Fine," she huffed out, "his views still haven't changed of what he expects out of a union - he wants the perfect Society wife, and I just can't be that."

"Wait, who said anything about marriage?"

She smiled tightly. "We're matched and have already been approved for the breeding programme," her tone was distasteful.

"What?" I spluttered.

"Yes," she surmised, "it was the basis of our fight - he went and got approval for it all before actually speaking to me. He deemed it romantic - I deemed it idiotic."

"Fuck," I said.

"Yes, fuck indeed, at least Ajax didn't deviate from his asshole persona - he did exactly what was expected of him."

"Yes," I sighed, "which only makes me an idiot."

"Aren't we all, Darling?" Raquel crooned. Standing tall, she raised her glass and declared a toast, "To being an idiot!" She shouted.

I could only raise my glass with a simple, "Cheers to that," because she was not wrong.

Raquel forced me out of my depressed bubble, pointing out new potential men and discussing her own sexual exploits in depth, making me blush and cringe simultaneously.

At work, she breezed in and out of my office, our firms working closely together as she meticulously mapped out and arranged a nationwide book tour that we would both be attending. And for the first time in a while, I was grateful that we would be travelling and not stationary, because it ultimately meant that there was little time for thoughts of Ajax SinClaire to consume me.

CHAPTER TWENTY-THREE : THE MEETUP

From the minute we arrived in Seattle, it was pouring. The rain came down in relentless sheets, making me long for a hotel room with an easy fire and a good book. Who knew? Perhaps Saxon and Saxon was rubbing off on me.

We were currently promoting the author's third book in a series, which meant that as a good employee of Saxon and Saxon, I took it upon myself to read the first two books in the series.

A slow burn fantasy with some love and intrigue provided the perfect escape, allowing me to not have to *think* about my life and the pangs of longing I felt when I least expected it. I wondered if he thought about me. If when he was in the shower, his hand wrapped around his cock - was it my name that rushed off of his lips?

Or was I being naive? Was it all one sided? I was making myself sick being this person, Ajax consuming my every thought. And so, I welcomed the travel; I welcomed Raquel's dirty stories; and I welcomed the workload.

Walking through the lobby of the hotel, I had no doubt that it was either Society owned or influenced. The level of luxury it exuded was absolute perfection. As we made our way to our respective rooms, we walked past a gym area, outfitted with large screens depicting naturistic scenery, and I suddenly realised that exercise had become such a big part of my everyday routine at the compound, that suddenly without it, I felt off-center.

I dumped my bags in my room and headed straight for the gym. Our first book signing was the following day, and the sudden urge to simply get on a treadmill with my music blaring in my ears was overwhelming. *This*, I thought - *this* is what I need to feel better - to feel more like myself.

I lost myself in the simple, monotonous pounding of my trainers against the rubber of the treadmill. The beat of Macklemore in my ear, as I exerted myself, needing to get rid of all the built up angst and pent up frustration that was simmering within. As much as I was irritated with Ajax, I was far angrier at The Society and what they subjected us to.

As I neared the end of my routine, resting to allow my heart rate to slow down, I looked up - the pull almost magnetic.

There, standing on the opposite side of the glass wall, was Ajax. He seemed as equally surprised to see me, his lips parted on an exhale.

Standing a few feet behind him were Joshua and Raquel - both smirking, and I knew that this run-in was hardly a coincidence.

He seemed to snap out of his trance, moving swiftly, stepping into the gym.

"How long are you here for?" He asked, his voice barely above a whisper.

"Two days," I spoke without moving, almost fearful that I would startle him. "You?" I tacked on.

"A week," he shrugged.

He looked good. Dressed in jeans and a tight fitting t-shirt that hugged his chest.

His gaze raked over my body, and the parts I had been willing myself to lie dormant suddenly sprang to life under his gaze.

"We doing this?" He asked, only it did not sound like a question.

"Are we?" I countered.

He smirked, glancing back towards Raquel and Joshua. "I think it's kind of expected, don't you?"

I pressed my lips into a thin line, "That depends on what the expectation is."

He stared at me for a moment. "You're angry," he stated, as if my anger were somehow a surprise to him.

I looked away quickly, in embarrassment. I was angry, but I also knew that my anger wasn't rational - not at him, anyway. In one swift move, he grabbed me by my arm and pulled me down the aisle.

"Excuse us," he called pleasantly over his shoulder at Josh and Raquel, "we need to talk. She's angry and I need to understand why she is so spitting furious at me."

Raquel barked a laughter of glee while I flipped her off.

"Ajax," I said his name in warning.

"I much prefer when you call me *Jax*," he smirked.

I glared at him.

"Jax, don't stop," he mimicked into my ear, "Harder, Jax."

I pushed away from him as he chuckled darkly.

We arrived outside my room and as soon as we stepped across the threshold; he had me pressed against the wall, his lips hovering above mine.

I hated that my body arched into him - that I *needed* him on such a basic, instinctual level.

"Why are you angry, Aria?" He demanded fiercely, his hand stroking my breast through my workout top.

I looked away angrily, refusing to give him the satisfaction of acknowledging that I was somehow hooked on him, and not being together was gutting me slowly.

"Have you missed me in the same way that I've missed you?" He purred, "Is that what has you all hot and bothered?"

"I won't be someone that you simply swipe right on," I snapped in irritation, overcoming the lust momentarily.

He pulled back slightly, his gaze seeking out my own.

"I haven't been with anyone since you," he spoke sincerely.

I frowned.

"But I will say," he grinned, leaning in to nip at my lip, "I fucking love seeing you jealous."

Before the protest could even leave my mouth, his lips were pressed against mine, and I had no more fight left within me to resist him. Because I wanted this and I had missed him.

I leaned into the kiss, biting down on his bottom lip in return. His groan set fire to my veins, and I needed him beneath me so fiercely that my lust for him scared me.

Not giving an inch, Ajax hoisted me up against his body and simply carried me across the room, depositing me on the bed.

He was right there with me the entire time, peeling my gym wear off of me in a heartbeat. He sank into me, and I exhaled deeply at the exquisite feel of him. I had no idea what this was - what it meant, but in this moment, in the here-and-now, it didn't matter.

Ajax began moving slowly, torturing me with his pumping movements that had me wrapping a fist into the front of his shirt, simply to pull him *closer*, to be *nearer*. He slid deeper inside of me willingly and it was all I could do to not throw my head back and scream his name.

Instead, I bit down on my lip, swallowing my moans, refusing to give him the satisfaction of me screaming his name.

Our breath mingled as he dipped his head closer towards mine.

"Say it," he growled.

I shook my head back and forth against the bed, unable to formulate words as he moved inside of me.

"Say my name," he urged, thrusting deeper within me. My inner walls began clenching around him as I started to shake, my climax building.

"No," I panted.

He increased his momentum and thrust into me harder, deeper, and faster.

"Jax," I screamed, my fingers fisting the bedsheets as I held on to the remainder of my sanity. "Oh God, Jax," I moaned, my hips rising to meet his thrusts, as he drove in deeper.

"Hold on," he ground out, and through the haze of my organsm, I dug my fingers into his back and held on as he released himself into me, the movements untamed.

As he rolled off of me, laying next to me panting, a smile played on the edge of his lips.

"What?" I demanded.

He turned his head to face mine, and the undiluted joy in his eyes caused my chest to stutter. He looked *happy*, and I realised that I had never seen Ajax look so joyous.

I shuddered, rolling on my side, my body seeking his to curl into.

"I didn't think I would see you again," I admitted softly.

"Neither did I."

The weight of what we left unsaid pressed in on us within the dimly lit room. It was as if, meeting him here, outside the confines of The Society, we were suddenly allowed to simply be Ajax and Aria - nothing more, nothing less.

"If we're doing this, I feel the incessant need to remind you that I don't share." I sat up, pulling my hair back away from my face.

Ajax broke out into a grin, and I ignored the way my stomach dipped at just the sight of him looking like that - hair tousled from sex, semi naked, and grinning at me like the idiot he was.

"Aria, honestly, I have been working ridiculous hours - there has been no time for me to even think of taking anyone else to my bed - even if I wanted to."

I glared at him.

"And, I didn't want to."

"And I'm just supposed to believe that?" I asked.

"Yes."

Silence hung between us once more, but not the uncomfortable kind.

"I love it when you look at me like that," he said seductively.

"Like what?" I couldn't tear my eyes from him.

"Like you are willing to claw up anyone that may have propositioned me," his eyes gleamed, "it's fucking sexy as hell."

Heat flooded my cheeks as I turned away quickly. "I don't play well with others."

"Most alphas don't," he said, kissing the top of my head as he dressed.

Raquel and I had decided to head downtown for drinks, but with Ajax and Joshua in town, naturally, they tagged along.

Joshua spread himself in the back of a booth, ordering a rack of ribs and a cheeseburger, whilst Ajax headed to the bar to fetch us a round of drinks.

"We've been in this place for five hours and already he's in a better mood," Joshua commented, biting into his burger.

"What do you mean?" I asked, whilst Raquel simply smirked.

"I mean, that since we left Austin, Ajax has been temperamental as hell, refusing to meet up with any woman, and working the employees into the ground."

"You're the VP now," I stated, "do something about it."

"I did," Josh ground out, Raquel breaking down into a fit of giggles, "I brought him to you. The two of you need to sort out whatever shit you have going on."

"Nothing major is going on. We simply have fun when we are together," I offered lamely.

"Yeah, and I'm Mother Theresa," he smirked.

Ajax chose that exact moment to arrive with a tray filled with drinks.

"What did I miss?" He asked, his eyes glancing at everyone around the table before settling on me.

I waited to see what Joshua offered. "We were just talking about how much *fun* you and Aria have together."

I rolled my eyes.

"Shut it, Josh," Ajax barked as he slid into the booth next to me.

His hand slid up my thigh discreetly beneath the table, and the doomsday rattling within my chest died down.

It turned out that Joshua and Ajax were in Seattle to aggressively buy out another tech firm. The deal was wrapped up, and they were simply here to sign off on the paperwork and meet the existing staff. Joshua and Raquel had been texting each other and somehow arranged our schedules to align. I couldn't be mad at Raquel - not really.

As the sun set, and it became evident that it was time to turn in, Ajax followed me to my room, showing me exactly how much his body had missed mine. We spent our nights together, exhausting ourselves in the best possible way, and during the day we both went our separate ways for work. Surprisingly, it didn't overwhelm me in the least.

On our last morning together, Ajax lifted me onto him, sliding himself deep within me, content to lie back and allow me to set the pace. It was slower, and somehow more erotic as I rocked back and forth on his cock. He cupped my breasts, pinched my nipples and played with my clit, urging me to tumble over the edge, and in my oblivion, I felt him jerk and spasm beneath me as he found his own pleasure.

I slumped on top of him, unwilling and unable to get off - to leave. He pulled me closer, kissing and nuzzling my neck, and I wondered how many others got to see this side of Ajax.

CHAPTER TWENTY-FOUR : THE OFFER

The cities we were visiting were becoming one big blur as Raquel and I ushered in the book signing, only to leave again.

Ajax and I had left on unspoken promises, with the understanding that we'd see each other again. I just didn't know when. Raquel tried to pester me about him, but I kept shutting her down. It's not that I didn't want to speak about him, it's just that I didn't know what to say.

I didn't know what Ajax and I were, or even what we could be. I had no idea what an *us* even looked like, only that it wasn't possible under The Society.

Raquel occasionally smirked and joked about where Ajax was in the world, so I knew that I'd see him again - if only because Raquel arranged it.

As Raquel and I were preparing the day's book signing, a shadow fell across our desk at the back of the Barnes and Nobles book store we were stationed in.

Sarah Lipson was standing before us, a smile on her face. Despite her small stature, her shadow was large and intimidating.

"Hello, ladies," she crooned.

Raquel smiled back weakly, whilst I was certain that my own smile resembled a grimace.

"Aria," she addressed me, "I have need of you - come," she commanded.

She turned on her heel, expecting me to follow. I had no choice as I glanced towards Raquel, who gave me a light shrug, and proceeded to follow her path.

She led me to a small coffee shop down the road, taking a seat as if she owned the place - and she probably did.

"Now," she spoke with a voice of authority, "I understand that you took a course in college on creative writing?"

My stomach settled, unsure of where exactly this conversation was heading.

"Ye-es," I dragged out the word, as if it would be less incriminating somehow.

"Good," she nodded to herself, ordering two cappuccinos with a flick of her wrist, "and now you're working at Saxon and Saxon, so you know more about the publishing process."

"Well, I know more than I did when I started, but I would hardly call myself an expert."

"Nonsense," she said, her hand reaching out for mine, "you just need to surround yourself with the right people - that is easily arranged."

Her hand felt oily and heavy against my skin, and I fought the urge to pull away.

"The Society has always operated in secret," she began, and this seems like a new train of thought entirely.

"I suppose," I shrugged.

"But at some point it will all come crashing down. Already the conspiracy theorists are skirting far too close to the truth."

I remained silent, understanding that she was not finished yet.

"When The Society is revealed for what we are, we need to ensure that we stand as the saviours. Do you understand what that means?"

I shook my head, panic clogging my throat.

"It means that we need to start shifting the narrative. It means that we need to start creating our own stories about The Society - around the very idea that The Society even exists - and put that out into the world. All in the form of movies, film and music. All fictional, of course - all depicting The Society as the hidden heroes of the world."

I looked at her as if she had lost her mind.

"So that when The Society is truly revealed," she continued, "it will be more palatable for the public to swallow - embrace even."

"Oka-ay," I dragged the word out, trying to make sense of what Sarah was saying.

"And that's where you come in. We need you to curate or write a fictional series around us - around all the good we have done - the necessity for a group like us to exist."

"But I'm not a writer," I spluttered, panicking.

"Then find a ghostwriter," she countered firmly.

"I don't know if I can do this," I implored.

Her face hardened.

"I understand that your father has the potential to be elected as chair of the National Gold Index Board," her voice lowered.

I blinked in surprise.

"Yes," she smiled cruelly, "we promote our members throughout the world. The thing about this position is that he needs to be seen as the perfect family man - no blemishes on his record, no family disputes, no leaked tapes from his daughter."

"What do you mean?" My fingers dug into the armrest of the chair as I fought to remain calm.

"Aria, Aria, Aria," she spoke as if chastising a child, "we still have all that video footage from you and Raul in the warehouse - or did you forget? Ajax's video cameras came in incredibly handy in the end."

My heart plummeted.

"You wouldn't," I gasped.

"Oh, we most definitely would." She arched a perfectly manicured brow at me.

My head was swimming with the sensation of betrayal. I knew that they weren't good. I knew that The Society blackmailed and manipulated people, and now I was experiencing it firsthand.

Did I care about my father's career? I didn't have to think about that question for long; the answer was a resounding no. Not really anyway. He had never been there for me. But this? This would break my mother. And, if I was being honest with myself - it would shatter me as well.

I felt my nausea rise, and for a minute I wanted to be sick. I wanted to vomit all over Sarah and her perfectly tailored suit. I wanted to puke all over The Society.

Instead, I swallowed down the bile that was resting uneasily in my stomach and said, "What do I have to do?"

Her lips curled back in pleasure, and I understood in that moment how dangerous The Society actually was.

"You have a few weeks to outline your story. You will need to come back to our compound for us to examine your plan and improve upon it - it shouldn't take more than a week, and then you can go back to your job and get it written and published."

"There's no guarantee that a publisher will pick it up," I said, knowing that I was grasping at straws.

"Don't worry about that," Sarah looked amused, "it will get published."

Without waiting for my reply, Sarah pushed off the table and was out the door within a heartbeat, leaving me to muddle through my thoughts of confusion.

Subliminal messaging - I was pretty sure that that was what this was. She was asking me to craft a story that showed The Society are the heroes. The problem with this is that I wasn't sure they were the heroes. Sarah had just blackmailed me by threatening to release the video of Raul fucking me whilst I was fulfilling my assignment for *them*.

I hated Sarah in that moment. I hated Sarah and Benson and everyone within The Society. Did Ajax know what his cameras would be used for? My stomach plummeted as I refused my thoughts to linger on him. They didn't give me a choice.

The book would be a work of fiction though, so hopefully those who read it would only view it as such, and nothing more. Perhaps it wouldn't even be that widely read? But as soon as that thought entered my mind, I had to discard it - The Society would ensure it was a bestseller.

On shaky legs, I stood up and made my way back towards the bookstore, back towards Raquel.

I had allowed myself to grow complacent, content in the idea that I had done my servitude and thus would be left alone from The Society. I knew I had been naive, but the sourness of it all left me reeling.

I found a trash can as I walked and heaved up the contents of my stomach as I processed exactly what I had agreed to and exactly what was threatened.

Without even thinking, I reached for my phone, dialling my mother.

She answered on the second ring, "Hello, Honey," she gushed, sounding happy to hear from me.

"Is Dad up for a chairman position on the Gold Board?" I demanded, forgoing a greeting.

Silence crackled down the line.

"Mom?"

"Yes," she breathed out, "he is, but that information is entirely confidential. Whatever they've asked of you, weigh up your options."

My heart stuttered. My mother knew. My mother knew exactly what they were about - what they were capable of. And she was speaking carefully in case this conversation was being monitored.

"I'll be careful," I promised, and hung up the phone.

Sarah had not been lying.

The bookstore was exactly the same as when I had left, nothing changed. I felt like I was drowning and the world around me didn't notice - couldn't see what was right in front of them.

Raquel gave me a questioning look, but I simply shook my head - I couldn't involve her, not when I was grappling for safety, and I wasn't even sure what that looked like.

CHAPTER TWENTY-FIVE : THE WHIRLWIND

Raquel knew something had occurred between Sarah and me, but we both chose to pretend like everything was completely fine.

I found myself in Austin once again, attending a gala held for the various publishing houses that Saxon and Saxon worked with. The shift of creatives moving to Texas saw the company take an unprecedented choice in hosting the gala here.

The cooler temperatures made the evening pleasant, and I wondered if I would ever be able to think of Austin without associating Ajax with it.

My green dress flowed beneath me, showing just the right amount of cleavage to be considered classical. The best feature of the gown, though, was undoubtedly the deep pockets that sat within my skirts.

I smiled politely at the guests, twirling my way through the crowd, Raquel chuckling behind me.

The bar was crowded, and I watched in awe and irritation as a man opened some space beside him.

I slid next to him, only to realise that he was now looking directly down the front of my dress.

"And here I thought a book party would be boring, and then a model arrived."

"I'm not a model," I snapped.

"That's probably by choice." He blew a ring of smoke towards my face.

"I'm Danzel," he smiled, and even though I found everything about him abhorrent, I liked him because he so clearly did not belong in this polished world.

"Danzel?" I laughed, "That seems like the name of a dancer."

"I've been called worse." He smiled, dimples appearing on both sides. "What are you drinking?"

"Nothing yet - which is the problem."

He barked a laugh, and before I could find out what Danzel was about to say next, large possessive hands slid around my waist from behind.

"No sharing, remember?" The seductive voice tickled my ear.

I arched back into him and ran my hand up his neck and across his five o'clock shadow.

My body ignited under his touch as he dragged me to the nearest adjoining room.

An empty coat closet welcomed us, and I did not care as he pressed me against the wall and deftly slid my panties off of me.

"We don't have a lot of time," he growled, lifting me onto a large wooden chest of drawers.

"Then make it quick," I said huskily.

My skirts billowed around us, and I heard the deep reverberating sound of my head hitting the back of the wall as he seated himself deep inside me with one swift thrust.

I moaned loudly, his wicked grin sending heat down my veins.

We heard the shuffle of feet and tickling of glasses from behind the door, both of us pausing for a moment as we allowed our gazes to track each other.

He looked good in a tux, his hair slightly ruffled as he bent towards me. I turned my head slightly, giving him access to my neck. He kissed and nipped, just above my collarbone and it was all I could do to simply hold on.

"These," he growled, "need to be naked and on top of me tonight." My breasts ached as he palmed a playful slap across them. I needed to feel his hands on my bare skin, and with that sheer thought alone, I was moving against him, moaning softly into his neck.

"Come for me, baby girl," he whispered, and as if his entire being commanded my body, I shattered against him. He held me firm as the universe exploded beneath my eyelids.

Thrusting in and out in me aggressively, I knew he was close. I bounced in time with his thrusts, my second orgasm causing me to gasp in surprise. I lost all sense of self and time as I clung to him as wave after wave of pleasure hit.

"Aria," he panted, "fuck."

And suddenly it was my turn to hold him, watching as his jaw clenched and his legs quivered as he came.

He deposited me gently against the wall, his large cock sliding out of me, causing me to whimper at the loss. He grinned wickedly. "We'll be doing more of this later."

He kissed my brow and suddenly was adjusting his tux and stepping through the door.

Fucking Ajax SinClaire blew my mind every time.

Asshole.

By the time I had straightened my clothing and stepped back into the gala room, Ajax was on stage, offering a speech to those in attendance as the key sponsor.

How I had missed that Molton Tech was the main sponsor for this, I had no idea, but looking at Raquel and Josh sitting closely to one another made me wonder how much Raquel had actually orchestrated.

Ajax's gaze glided over the audience in attendance, finally resting on me.

"The importance of stories and the characters within them cannot be highlighted enough," he began, a slow hush descending upon the crowd.

"Is that *the* Ajax SinClaire?" Someone near me gasped.

I ignored them as I stood on the outskirts of the room, watching him command everyone's attention.

"One character can upturn everything within an existing narrative," he paused dramatically, his stare held mine captive, "and," he released me from his gaze, "the same can be said for an investment. It is with great pleasure that I stand before you today as the key sponsor for this event. I would like to take this time to further announce that Molton Tech will be sponsoring two million dollars annually towards new upcoming writers that these fine publishing houses deem fit."

The room broke out into wild applause, and once more Ajax's gaze sought me out.

The gala event was the type of function that seemed to drag out too long in some places and seemed to be over within a blink of an eye in others.

Raquel and Josh disappeared together, and I tried to pretend as if I did not notice. When I left the event, Ajax was still in a deep discussion with one of the presidents of a large publishing firm, and I did not want to be that girl that hung around uncertainly for a man.

My hotel room was warm as I stripped off the emerald green gown. My breasts were sensitive from the promise of being touched. Refusing to allow my longing to rise to the surface, I threw on a Clash t-shirt and prepared for bed.

A soft knocking sounded at my door. I hoped Joshua hadn't hurt Raquel. Did I have wine in the mini-bar fridge? Wine was for heartbreak, right? I opened the door just a crack to see that it wasn't Raquel.

Ajax stood in the hallway, looking devilishly handsome. He had long since lost his jacket, and his top shirt button was undone. I pressed my thighs together, and I wasn't sure if it was due to nerves or anticipation.

"You going to let me in, Aria?"

The way he rolled my name off of his lips shifted my concentration, until all I could envision was myself on top of him, naked and bare.

Wordlessly, I stepped aside, giving him a wide berth of entry.

As if sensing my nerves, he grabbed my hand and pulled me closer towards him. His tongue parted my lips, and with his mouth upon mine, I suddenly did not feel so confused anymore.

His shirt came off first, his pants followed, and then he was guiding us to the bed. He laid down first, allowing me to straddle him.

"I missed this," he said, playing with the hem of my t-shirt.

"You mean me in just my t-shirt?"

He smiled wistfully, "It's what you wore when we used to watch series."

My heart twisted as I sat above him, looking into his eyes. We could pretend that this thing between us wasn't real or that it didn't matter, but we both knew the truth. Without The Society, things would be so much simpler. I knew that I would experience my first heartbreak, and it didn't matter if it was because of Ajax or The Society. I knew intrinsically that it would happen. Because somewhere the lines had blurred and I had caught feelings for him, and sitting atop of him, watching him as he watched me, I knew that he felt the same.

I did the only thing I could. I lifted the shirt over my head, revealing my breasts, and sank onto him, allowing him to slide deep within my soul.

When I moved against him, our eyes locked, his fingers gripped my hips firmly, but never once did he push for me to quicken my pace, as if we were both content to simply feel one another, prolonging this moment.

"Jax," I whispered, moaning in a way that told him that the sensations were *too* much, that I was feeling *too* much.

"I got you," he whispered, flipping me onto my back, sinking deep as he took control.

I found myself as my legs wrapped around his waist, moaning and panting into his neck, clawing at his back.

"Aria," he grunted, "my Aria."

And then he was tumbling down right beside me, and there was a rightness to that that had me cupping his jaw and leaning over to kiss him.

We made love throughout the night, neither of us content to sleep. When morning rolled around, Ajax was still moving deep within me.

"I fucking hate leaving," he whispered.

And it was because of that haunted look in his eyes that I flipped us over, slid on top, and rode him into oblivion. I wanted to make him forget - even if just for a moment. As his hands cupped my breasts, we spiralled into euphoria together.

We both flew out of Austin that day - back to our respective lives and locations, and this time, I knew that the ache that I felt from being apart from him was reciprocated. Knowing that, however, did not make me feel better.

I pulled my coat tighter, shielding myself from the cold Colorado wind. Raquel and I had flown in the previous day, and I was grateful that we were on the last leg of this book tour. I'd have to go back to the compound for a week when I returned, and while that had my stomach in a tangle of nerves, I still thought it would be more stable being in one location.

Every time I thought of The Society and the blackmail, I would puke, sometimes simply dry-heaving, at the realisation of the extent that they used people.

My heeled boots wobbled slightly on the cobble stoned streets, but I made it back to the hotel in one piece.

A dark, ominous figure sat in the hotel lobby, scowling at all who walked by. And, apparently, he was waiting for me.

"What are you doing here?"

"We need to talk," Ajax ground out.

I ushered him to my room where he slammed the door with such force, the wall rattled. Clenching his fists, he turned to me.

"This *thing* that you're doing for The Society - the books that you're creating for them," he swallowed, as if battling with himself, "walk away from it Aria, leave them alone."

Anger surged within.

"I can't," I spat, "I can't just 'walk away'," I mimicked him, "it's not like they gave me that option."

He closed his eyes as if in pain.

"What are they blackmailing you with?" He croaked.

He knew what they were capable of and that was worry that I saw shining through his eyes.

"It doesn't matter," I said, deflated, "telling you won't change anything. Besides, I'm pretty sure it's going to be your donation that is going to fund the whole thing."

"I know," he ground out, "I fucking know. And this is my goddamn *punishment.*"

Shock skittered through me.

"Punishment for what?"

"Because I used my own goddamn money to *buy* you from Raul, even after they told me that if the price was too high to simply walk away, but I couldn't fucking leave you there. So I had to pledge my own fucking money to this project of theirs - but you were never supposed to be a part of it, not again."

Tears began filling my eyes as I shook my head in understanding.

"Walk away from this deal with them Aria," he begged.

"I can't," I sobbed.

"What do they have on you?"

I shook my head, stepping forward to sob onto his shirt. I couldn't tell him. It wasn't his fault and he would only shoulder more guilt.

"I wish things were different," he said, kissing my forehead gently, making his way down to my jaw.

"I wish we could run away," I whispered back.

He made love to me. Thoroughly.

"Are your breasts getting bigger?" He asked as we lay sated on the bed, his finger circling my nipple.

"No," I frowned, "they just look bigger because I've lost weight."

A look of concern flashed across his face as his lips found mine, once more, "Eat more," he commanded, just before his tongue slid into my mouth, clashing against my own.

Ajax flew out that afternoon, a prisoner to The Society, just as I was.

CHAPTER TWENTY-SIX : THE DISCOVERY

We were finally done with the book tour, and while I was grateful for that, I was nervous to spend another week under the watchful eyes of The Society.

Would Ajax be there? I didn't know. In a world filled with technology, we didn't even have each other's numbers. He owned a tech company, yet we didn't even text or call. It was as if by avoiding the normal interactions that those in a relationship portrayed, we - ourselves, could then say that we were not in a relationship.

My father had landed the role of Chairman, and truthfully, no one in our family was surprised - we were all towing the line with The Society. But, as such, my parents were out of town for his welcoming function, which just so happened to be on the same day as the annual Small Business Awards in Texas that my parents sponsored each year. And so naturally, I had to step in for the welcoming speech and to hand out the last award of the evening - all as a representative of the O'Luc family. In a way, the awards ceremony would act as a slight reprieve, delaying me marginally from The Society compound.

I watched the coffee swirl from a dark brown to a few shades lighter as I stirred in my cream. How badly did The Society need these fictional pieces? How terrible was their public image that they believed fictional pieces would help their cause. Unease settled within me, as with anything, there was often a grain of truth within the tale. The Society did terrible things - I knew that. Even Ajax had tried to warn me - tried to get me to leave this new project of theirs alone. I suppose this is what my life would be like - never free, not truly, because there would always be another project or assignment that I would need to complete for them. The aroma of coffee wafted towards me, curdling my stomach. I bolted for the bathroom, heaving up my previous meal.

"You know," Raquel murmured from the doorway, having followed my bolting figure, "you haven't been able to stomach coffee for over a week now."

I looked up at her, splashing water on my face.

"Do you want to get a test?" she asked, concern etching along her face.

"No," I shook my head, "I'm on the pill."

She pressed her lips together, displeasure seeping from her pores.

"The Society controls our birth control, so let's just be safe and get a test."

I stared at her in bewilderment. This wasn't possible. This couldn't be possible.

"What does this mean?" I stuttered, dumbfounded.

She looked at me sadly. "I don't know, they probably figured out that you and Ajax are together. It wouldn't surprise me, really."

Glancing around, she suddenly looked skeptical. "It's not safe to talk here, let's go and get you a test."

We power walked down the street, arm-in-arm. To the world, we looked like two friends on a coffee date, but the turmoil churning within was crippling.

"I'm fairly certain that you and Ajax are a match in the breeding programme," she huffed under her breath as a bus drove past, drawing out all other noise, "and them tampering with your birth control is their way of forcing you and Ajax together."

A wave of dizziness overcame me. "Ajax doesn't want this."

"Ajax doesn't know what he wants," Raquel snapped, "all he knows is what he *doesn't* want - and that's to not be controlled by The Society."

My eyes snapped up at hers.

"Don't look at me like that," she commanded, "I'm not thrilled to be part of them either."

How was it possible that so many of us were this unhappy? How did they still hold the reins of control?

The answer was sickeningly simple: blackmail and fear.

Raquel came out of the CVS with a brown paper packet filled with three different pee-on-the-stick type of tests. My whole world was crumbling, and all I could think was *this couldn't be happening.* I had done everything right. I had towed the line. I was jumping through their hoops. *This could not be happening.*

Raquel sat with me as we both stared at each stick - all of them showing two highlighted lines - all of them positive.

"I think," Raquel cleared her throat, "that if Ajax allows himself to be, he'll be a great father."

My chest caved in on itself as I sobbed. I sobbed for the lack of choice. I sobbed for the lack of freedom I had. And I sobbed because this baby would be born into The Society, and I was terrified.

Raquel hugged me tightly, fierce in her friendship.

"We're going to break free from them," she whispered in my ear, and I didn't know what her plan was, but I desperately needed to hold on to something, so I believed her.

Hope was a dangerous thing, but not having it was more terrifying.

We sat in silence for a long time, Raquel simply allowing me to come to terms with the way my life had suddenly shifted overnight. In that tiled bathroom cubicle, our friendship solidified - she saw how terrified I was to have a baby within The Society, and I in turn knew that she wanted to break free from them just as badly as I did.

A baby, I marvelled. Ajax and I had made a baby. The thought almost made me giddy. I wondered if it would be a boy or a girl. If it would inherit his gold-flecked eyes and charisma, or if it would look more like me. What a concept it was to create a child, to be responsible for shaping a person - their morals and beliefs, to be the pillar that guided them into the world, encouraging them at every turn.

My hand splayed across my stomach, as if I could protect this being of light from the outside world through sheer will.

I didn't want to be part of The Society, but perhaps if Ajax and I stopped running from this *thing* between us, we could make it work. Maybe we could be a family, even with the shadow of The Society looming over us.

Resolved, I glanced up at Raquel, her own expression pensive.

"Ajax has been trying to avoid the breeding programme for as long as I've known him. I think it was the only way he could truly rebel against his father."

"What do you mean?"

"They made him do deplorable things Aria, they turned him into their soldier at the age of fifteen. These last few weeks he has been the happiest I have seen him in a long time."

I frowned at her.

"I've known him and Joshua since we were all kids. Ajax never used to be such an asshole - he never used to be so guarded, and you have made him open up again. His initial reaction may not be one of excitement and joy, but this baby is a gift - even under the weight of The Society. Try and remember that, okay?"

I nodded, a lump forming in my throat that I seemed to struggle swallowing past.

"You and Josh have known each other since you were kids?"

She shrugged. "Some may have even dubbed us best friends," she smiled wryly.

"In all the time I've known you, you failed to mention that," I said blandly.

Raquel's barked laughter was joyous, easing the tension in my chest.

"Well, now you know," she stuck her tongue out at me playfully.

A flurry of questions bubbled up inside of me. I deftly pushed them down, knowing that when Raquel wanted to open up, I would be here.

"God, I hate you," she groaned.

"What? Why?" I demanded.

"You've just thrown up, found out you're pregnant and you still looked incredible. You'd probably look amazing in a plastic bag," she gagged, "model material. You would blend in in Cape Town with all the models on the beach."

As she spoke, there was a gleam in her eye, as if she were trying to convey a message that she was hoping I'd pick up.

I smiled at her, and I nodded. I felt braver, somehow, leaving that bathroom cubicle.

Raquel and I flew out separately, with me heading to Texas for the small business awards. We promised to text, but Raquel being Raquel, gave me fair warning that our messages were probably being screened, so I shouldn't send anything "idiotic."

As I chose a simple, black elegant gown for the business awards, and as I ran my hand across my stomach, I knew that I didn't look any different, but somehow everything had changed.

I stood in the wings of the stage, waiting for everyone to take their seats so that I could welcome everyone and introduce the MC. I had a unique position in that I could see the crowd, but they could not see me.

Large broad shoulders in a charcoal tailored suit drew my eye. A blonde dressed in a white dress that kept little to the imagination. She flung herself into him, arms wrapping around his neck, and for a moment I felt a pang of jealousy. She lifted her head towards his, mouth pressed upon his lips. As the music sounded, the cue for my entrance, the blonde unwrapped herself from the broad-shouldered man, and as he turned to take his place, it was Ajax's face that swivelled towards the table.

My heart plummeted. Loud ringing sounded in my ears, and I could not tell if the nausea rising within was due to the pregnancy or the betrayal.

I turned away, stunned, to find Josh standing a few feet away from me, handing a large cheque to one of the organisers - sponsorship money, no doubt.

"It's not what it looks like," he uttered, seeing my paled complexion.

"I don't want to hear it," I said, surprised at how steady my voice sounded in my ears. Pivoting on my heels, I walked onto the stage and proceeded with professionalism, deliberately not making eye contact with Ajax, skipping over his table as I glanced at the crowd.

As the business awards ended and slowly bled into the after-drinks function, I slipped away, content to be left alone, unsure if I wanted Ajax to come and find me.

I was such a fucking idiot. How many times had he told me that he doesn't dabble with Society girls? Had I honestly believed that we were in a relationship because the sex had changed? Yes, I had, which only made me angrier at myself.

He had been right all along; I was just a naive little girl.

Cradling my stomach, I whispered, "It's going to be you and me, little one, just you and me."

Ajax did not seek me out. I fell asleep alone, angry and crying. Of course, I blamed it on the hormones. But in the light of day, with his side of the bed still cold, I promised myself that I would not shed another tear over Ajax fucking SinClaire. This baby needed me to be strong, and so that's what I would be.

I dressed, my chest heavy but my mind clear, and took the long drive back to the Austin compound.

I was nervous to be going back, but this time, I wasn't the naive girl that had stepped through the gates, afraid of what she would find. This time I knew that they were not inherently good, and I knew not to fall for the lies that spewed from Sarah Lipson's mouth.

CHAPTER TWENTY-SEVEN :
THE CONFRONTATION

The lobby was exactly as I remembered it, full of smiling Society members, all working for the organization in some way or form.

"Miss O'Luc," the woman with the clipboard smiled. "Mr. Benson and Miss Lipson have been expecting you. They will be in meeting room F4 at three o'clock this afternoon. Until then, you can relax as you choose."

I smiled in thanks, fairly certain that it looked like a grimace. As if I could possibly relax here, knowing what they did.

I found myself seated at one of the outside restaurant tables overlooking the pool. It was as if my brain was working on autopilot, ordering my usual off the menu.

It was only when my order arrived that I realised my mistake. Coffee steamed seductively from my mug, sending waves of nausea rolling through me.

And wouldn't you know, sitting at the bar, with his back facing towards me, was Ajax. He was like a disease that I couldn't shake.

The heavy aroma of coffee wafted towards me as an icy breeze blew through the restaurant. That is all it took to have me bolting towards the bathroom.

I knelt in the small cubicle, heaving up the small amount I had eaten earlier. It was such a strange feeling to suddenly have an adverse reaction to something I had been consuming my entire adult life.

Hands shaking, I splashed water on my face, and finally emerged from the bathroom.

Standing outside the restrooms, stood Ajax, one leg hiked up against the wall, waiting for me.

I wiped my mouth against my sleeve, hoping that he could not detect the lingering scent of vomit.

"How long have you known?" He ground out, the golden specks of his eyes flashing angrily.

I wanted to deny what he suspected or knew, but I simply couldn't, and so I offered him the truth.

"A few days."

"Were you going to tell me?" He looked torn.

I contemplated my answer. "Before the business awards? Yes."

"And after?"

"I don't think it matters anymore Ajax," I replied coolly.

"It fucking matters," he snapped, his fist connecting with the wall. The bar staff's attention snapped towards us.

"We need to talk," he hissed.

"So talk," I countered.

"Not here."

"I have a meeting at three," I shrugged.

"I'll come to you after your meeting."

We stared at each other, his scowl increasing with each breath we took.

"Fine," I said, making my way towards the meeting with Benson and Sarah.

Some of my anger seemed to dissipate the closer I got to the meeting room. The hallway was eerily silent. A prickle of unease spread across my spine. I made a concerted effort to not touch my stomach. The last thing I needed was for The Society to discover that I was pregnant when I myself didn't know what I was going to do about it.

Since discovering that I was nurturing and growing another life, my hand seemed to find its way to my stomach naturally.

Benson and Sarah watched me carefully as I walked in, making my hairs stand on end.

"All right," Sarah snapped, "show us the story outline you have."

I silently slid my proposal across the table without looking up. She scrutinized the paperwork in front of her, frowning.

"There's no mention or even allusion to kidnapping or human trafficking of any kind in this," she snapped.

"Um… what?" I spluttered.

"Is she dense?" Sarah turned to Benson, belittling me in a way that angered and embarrassed me.

When Benson didn't reply, she turned towards me, "we need to be deemed as the heroes when it comes to human trafficking," she spat.

"Ok-ay?"

"We need to make sure that when people discover what we've been doing, that they don't question why we moved those girls, they simply assume that we saved them," she elaborated.

My mind spun into a fog as I struggled to keep up with what she was saying.

"The girls?" I said, my mind reeling.

"Oh for fuck sake," Sarah exploded, and the fact that prim Sarah Lipson was swearing was what shocked me out of my state, "you cannot possibly believe that we *saved* those women."

Her eyes widened in disbelief as she shook her head, laughing cruelly. She glanced at Benson and then back towards me.

"I'm going to lay it out for you. We took those girls for our own profit. Selling people is the largest black market industry and we are the biggest players in the field. Soldero picked up the girls for us, but somewhere along the line he got it into his thick skull that he would make more money *keeping* them, than handing them over to us - as initially agreed."

"You didn't save them?" I knew I was going into some sort of state of shock.

"No, Aria," she smiled, "*You* didn't save them."

I looked towards Benson, who simply shrugged his shoulders and said, "It's only business, Aria. We've been doing this for years."

"Now," Sarah clicked her fingers in the air, "back to the matter at hand. I expect revisions on this proposal within three days."

I sat, staring blankly, unable to respond. Could I turn them in for human trafficking? Was I an accomplice? If it was just me, I wouldn't hesitate, but now there was someone else dependent upon me, and I wouldn't leave my baby at the mercy of The Society.

"How can you live with yourself knowing that you are bartering away young girls' lives?" I demanded, "How could you lead me to believe that I was *saving* them?" I shouted, my voice growing louder in volume.

"Easy," she hissed, leaning across the table. "I can easily do it because those actions ensure the survival of our organisation. I didn't see you acting so high and mighty when it was *slavery* that placed your family in the position that they're in today! This is no different."

I swallowed the bile working its way up in my throat.

"We are *selling* people!" I implored.

"And we will continue to do so," she slammed her hand on the table, staring at me.

"I think," Benson intervened, "that you should go and revise your proposal and we can reconvene in a few days."

He spoke professionally, as if we were discussing the stock exchange. I stood up, my legs shaking beneath my weight, and left, stumbling down the hallway.

I vomited in the nearest bathroom, and this time I knew it had nothing to do with my pregnancy. I had debased myself, posed as a brothel prostitute, and had played a role in the murder of Soldero's men and wife. I had *assisted* in the sale of human beings. My stomach heaved once more. How many people had died at their hands?

This was how they maintained control, because after being an accomplice to such incorrigible acts, I could not leave The Society now, because they would quite easily spin this in a way that I would take the fall for these crimes should I choose to leave.

How many other crimes were they a part of? How many women and children went missing under their watch?

And just when I thought my stomach couldn't sink any further, I wondered if Ajax knew? Josh? Dr. Leila Oswaldo?

How many people had deceived me? How deep did the rot run? My mind was connecting dots that weren't there, imagining the absolute worst of everybody. Raquel? No, I knew that she stood against what The Society was doing. I found my resolve and forced myself to leave the public bathroom.

My shaky legs carried me all the way to my room, where Ajax was sitting slumped against my door.

"What's wrong?" He demanded, standing up swiftly.

My ashen face and shaking hands gave me away.

CHAPTER TWENTY-EIGHT : RUN

He opened the door, ushering me in first. Stepping into the room was a dèjá vu moment, realising that we had indeed come full circle.

I walked to the kitchen and grabbed a glass of water.

"What happened?" He pressed, worry creasing his brow. I didn't want his concern, and so I held on to my anger, reminding myself that he was an asshole.

"Human trafficking," I croaked, looking up at him.

"They told you," he sounded deflated, and that one sentence confirmed everything. I exploded.

"Yes, they fucking told me!" I yelled, stabbing a finger into my chest, "Sarah *told* me exactly how I had *assisted* them in their human trafficking endeavour!"

He didn't step away from my rage, instead he simply looked at me, sadness creeping in.

"Do they know about…" he trailed off, his fingers brushing my stomach.

"Don't," I ground out, "Don't pretend you care - not after the business awards."

"It wasn't like that," he snapped, "and of course I fucking care - I've been *caring* for a long time now!" The flecks in his eyes glowed golden. He stepped closer, his senses crowding in on mine. "Do they know?" He whispered.

"No," I swallowed, "and you shouldn't care either."

"The woman I went with was Olga Rosenberg. She is notorious for kissing all her dates as a publicity stunt."

I stared at him.

"Don't believe me?" He huffed, "Google it."

"Why didn't you come and find me then?" I asked softly.

He gripped the back of his neck, shifting in his place uncomfortably. "Because Josh advised me not to. He said that I should let you cool off."

"And you listened to Josh?" I asked, flabbergasted.

"I don't know what I'm doing when it comes to you, so yes, I listened to fucking Josh. In hindsight, it wasn't my finest moment."

My breath shuddered out of me. He hadn't betrayed me, not in the initial way I had thought.

"Listen to me," he whispered, his thumb lifting my chin towards his face. "Do you know what these people are capable of?"

I swallowed down the lump in my throat, somehow knowing that what he was about to say was going to be so much worse than I could ever imagine.

"I'm in too deep, they own my soul, have samples of my blood," he smiled self-deprecatingly, "but you and *this*," his fingers brushed my stomach, firmer this time, "have a chance to get out."

I stared at him in shock.

"You need to run," he whispered, kissing my forehead. "You and I both know that this baby deserves better than this."

I began shaking my head in denial, but he simply smiled at me, and that smile shattered my heart a million times over.

"I didn't want to like you, you know? Because I knew that you would get under my skin and set fire to my soul. Let me do this, let me protect my *family.*"

I closed my eyes as the onslaught of emotions lashed at me.

"Run," he whispered into my ear, "run and create a phenomenal life for the two of you."

"What about you?" I asked, swallowing down the sob that was building.

Wariness shuttered across his face, "They own me, Aria, and they will make me hunt you, so if you ever see me again, you should run."

"No," the sob broke free, "no," I repeated, "no!" I screamed.

He pulled me closer to his chest, his large arms wrapping around my back.

"I want you to know," he said softly, "that in the end, if it was up to me, I would have chosen you, anyway."

A cried into his chest, shaking my head at the words he was saying.

"I want you to know, that I would give anything for it to be the three of us," he smoothed back my hair as my sobs grew fiercer, "but I also want you to know that because of them, because of the things that I have done, I am not a good man, but being with you made me want to *try*." His voice cracked on the last word.

"You need to run," he said, more urgently this time. "They don't know that you're pregnant and they don't have their claws fully in you yet, so run far away from here and *live.*"

"Can't you come with us? We could go to -"

"Don't," he growled, cutting me off, "don't tell me where you are going to go because if they suspect I know, there are all sorts of ways that they can get that information out of me."

My fists clenched into his shirt out of absolute desperation. "I don't want to leave you," I whispered my confession into his chest.

"Shhhhh," he smiled down at me. "You're going to be fine," he promised.

We held each other in silence until it felt as if I had no more tears to spill.

"Why will they make you hunt me?" I glanced up at him hesitantly, and for the first time, Ajax looked lost.

"Because I am next in line to take over the organisation, and you were set up to be my match."

"What?" I gasped.

"It doesn't matter now," he answered, stroking my back in smooth, luxurious patterns.

"That's why you didn't want to date anyone in The Society," I said, the pieces finally clicking into place. "You didn't want to give them an heir."

He grimaced. "It was the only way I could rebel," he confessed.

We made love for the last time, my heart breaking with each thrust, as he gave himself over to me over and over again. And as he lay in a deep sleep next to me, my palm above his chest, watching the rise and fall of each breath, I knew that he was right - I needed to run, for our baby, I needed to run.

I snuck out, padding lightly on bare feet, and there was a moment where Ajax's breathing shifted, indicating that he might be awake. But neither of us said anything, and he didn't turn around, so I simply slipped out the door.

EPILOGUE : CAPE TOWN

It was windier than I had expected, but as beautiful as all the photographs I had scoured online.

Mansions dotted the coastline of Camps Bay, peppered with trendy and expensive restaurants and venues. And in a weird way, because of all of these material reasons, it felt *familiar*, putting me at ease.

I sunk my legs deeper into the sand; the sunset teasing those who braved the windy beach. Raquel hadn't lied. This place was crawling with beautiful bodied models, which meant that no one really gave me a second look.

And for the first time… ever, I was free. And I had absolutely no idea what to do with that freedom, but I had promised Ajax that I would *live*. My hand rested upon my stomach as I breathed in the salty air and thought about what that exactly meant. The eye of my tattoo stared out at the ocean, and the mix of possibilities was enough to weigh me down. I shook off my anxiety and reminded myself to enjoy the moment - it was no longer simply myself that I needed to look out for.

You can read more about Aria and Ajax, and The Society, in the next book in this series:

The Firm

THANK YOU

Two words that are so simple, yet express so much.

Melissa - you have been a godsend. Thank you for reading and supporting.

Hannah - thank you for loving this story, despite its darkness.

Emelia - my lief! You are my ride or die. No words can express how grateful I am to you - truly.

Enrico, Augusto and Giovanna - my safe and wild place. You are my constant. Thank you for embracing my chaos. I love you three more than words can possibly express.

To the readers and supporters - thank you for reading, engaging and supporting. Truly, none of this would be possible if there was no one to read my work.

And the ricers. Thank you for not shying away as I vented and discussed certain scenes. Thank you for encouraging me to explore this writing tick - this book was written in between projects in a wild flurry. There is something so special about our group and even if you are not aware, you encourage me to do better - force me to write more, and for that I am grateful.

OTHER WORKS BY ERIN MC LUCKIE MOYA

Printed in Great Britain
by Amazon

23268534R00089